THE MULTI-MAN

Research biologist Jeffrey Dexter's experiments produce a creature capable of endless reproduction, yet lacking human reserve. Then he's murdered — swept aside by the ruthless Multi-Man. Dexter's wife's claim, that the new Jeffrey Dexter is only a cellular duplicate of her husband, finds her incarcerated in an institution for the mentally unbalanced. Dexter No 2 develops his plans: famous people are duplicated to nominate Dexter's Presidency in a new scientific era. Can Scotland Yard Detective Sergeant Hanbuy hold him back?

JOHN RUSSELL FEARN

THE MULTI-MAN

Complete and Unabridged

LINFORD
Leicester

First published in Great Britain

First Linford Edition
published 2010

British Library CIP Data

Fearn, John Russell, *1908 –1960.*
The multi-man. - - (Linford mystery library)
1. Human cloning- -Fiction.
2. Science fiction.
3. Large type books.
I. Title II. Series
823.9′12–dc22

ISBN 978–1–44480–105–7

Published by
F. A. Thorpe (Publishing)
Anstey, Leicestershire

Set by Words & Graphics Ltd.
Anstey, Leicestershire
Printed and bound in Great Britain by
T. J. International Ltd., Padstow, Cornwall

This book is printed on acid-free paper

1

Secret experiment

To the world in general, and his wife in particular, Jeffrey Dexter was an organic chemist — which is to say he was employed in the Central London Laboratories, entirely Government controlled, as an analyst in foodstuffs, cosmetics and the hundred and one other commodities which constantly reach the public. Even the gum to be used on envelopes came within his province, and as far as it went he was expert enough at his job — expert enough, anyway, to put aside enough money to build for himself a small, isolated laboratory on a derelict site in the centre of the city. And what he did here was nobody's business. Indeed, even his wife did not know anything about it — until she found out one evening by accident,

She found out because her taxi

happened to stop at the traffic lights. It was not unnatural that her gaze wandered idly about her whilst she waited for the taxi to move on, and it was in the process of this survey that she beheld her husband leaving a small, long building of ferrocrete only about fifty yards away. She recognised him in a moment — and being a woman of action she promptly left the taxi, paid the driver, then hurried after her husband as he ambled towards the nearest underground station. From his manner it was plain he was lost in thought; so much so he hardly seemed to recognise his wife even when she was confronting him.

'Surprised, Jeff?' she enquired.

'A bit,' he admitted. 'Where did you spring from?'

'A taxi back on the main road there. I've been spending a hit of time with Claire, knowing you'd be working overtime this evening, then I took a taxi back so I could get supper ready for you in time.'

'Very kind of you, dear,' Jeffrey Dexter smiled. 'Now we can go home together.'

'Surely — when you've explained yourself.'

Jeffrey looked vaguely surprised, not so much at his wife's remark as at the frustrated anger in her hazel eyes. She was a good-looking girl of twenty-five, blonde haired and trim figured, very much in love with her husband and her home, but humanly angry just the same when she felt she had been taken advantage of — which was exactly as she felt at the moment.

'Explain myself?' Jeffrey repeated. 'Concerning what?'

'It's no use you trying to fool mc, Jeff. I saw you come out of that building back there — and it certainly isn't any part of the Central London Laboratories. Or is it?'

'No,' Jeffrey admitted frankly. 'But I have been working overtime, on my own account.'

'Oh — I see.' Helen Dexter came slowly to a halt as they walked slowly along together.

'In fact I've been working overtime for about two years now. I was going to tell you about it finally when I had something worthwhile to offer. Since you've apparently forestalled me you may as well know all about it. That building back there is mine. I bought it.'

'Why? Couldn't we do with the extra money in the home instead of throwing it away on a dismal-looking place like that?'

Jeffrey threw back his head and laughed, and it was singular to him that when he laughed he thoroughly enjoyed it and made a great deal of noise. It was highly infectious, too, and made it nearly impossible for Helen to maintain her suspicious attitude. That was the trouble with Jeffrey: when he laughed he changed from a serious young man of thirty into an irresponsible schoolboy. With his tumbling dark hair and good-humoured face it was impossible in these moments to be angry with him.

'I don't think I said anything funny,' Helen objected.

'But you did, without knowing it. That building back there may look dismal from the outside, but that's no guide. Within it are scientific instruments that many experts would give their souls to possess!'

'And where in the world did you get the money to buy such things? Scientific instruments — worthwhile ones anyway — cost a fortune.'

'Brand new ones do, certainly, but these have been constructed from surplus government stock, to which I have easy access at very low prices. You know the sort of things — old transformers, switchboards, vacuum tubes, potentiometers — '

'All of which must have cost a certain amount of money. No use trying to get away from that.'

'Very little. I knew how to go about the job. In any case,' Jeffrey continued seriously, 'it's a well-tried axiom that if you want to accumulate you must speculate, and I'm making something in that laboratory there which will be worth a fortune when it's finished.'

Helen looked at him seriously for a moment and then sighed.

'What, for instance?'

'Come back to the lab and I'll show you.'

Jeffrey took her arm possessively and led her back down the street. When they reached the ferrocrete building she stood watching in some wonder as he carefully operated a complicated time-switch on the massive entrance door.

'Why all the palaver?' she asked curiously.

'Because of the value of the stuff inside. It is not the common thief I fear, but possible agents of scientists who may have some idea of what I'm up to. Some of them — the more ambitious types — would go to any length to get their hands on the basis of my discovery. That's why, and I'm the only one who knows how to unfasten it before the time limit has expired. I'd set it for tomorrow evening, of course.'

'And more overtime work?'

'Naturally. Might as well employ myself usefully in what spare moments I do get — Ah! That's got it.'

With a click the door lock responded and Jeffrey pushed the door inwards on its massive hinges. In the bright sunlight of the June evening Helen noticed that the door was immensely thick and lined on the inside with some kind of insulated material. The door hinges too had been fitted into specially devised stone structures. So much Helen had time to notice, then Jeffrey closed the door behind her and total darkness descended.

'No windows,' came his voice out of the void. 'It not only saved building costs, but it also makes it tougher for any would-be intruder to get in. Windows can always be circumvented by an experienced thief.'

Light appeared abruptly from four big overhead lamps, and Helen looked about her in wonder. The laboratory itself was not particularly large, or else it was that there was so much equipment in it that it seemed smaller than it really was.

'Plenty of stuff here, anyway,' Helen said at length, moving forward and contemplating baffling apparatus. 'You'll have to explain it to me, Jeff. I don't know a thing about science.'

'Probably be more to the point if I explained what I'm trying to do. Here, take a seat.'

Jeffrey pulled forth a stool, settled her

upon it. 'You're probably not going to believe me even when I do tell you,' he said, thinking.

'Try me out and see.'

'All right, then; here it is neat. I'm making a duplicate of myself.'

Helen stared, then she asked slowly: 'And that is going to make us a fortune? I don't want to sound rude, Jeff, but would anybody want a duplicate of you? It isn't as though you're important like a Prime Minister or somebody famous.'

Jeffrey gave that shattering laugh of his, and at length it petered out in a sigh.

'The odd slant you do get on things, Helen! Wonder if all women are like you?'

'Never mind what women are like: what precisely are you doing?'

'I'll take it step by step,' Jeffrey decided. 'In the first place you'll be aware of the elementary fact, I suppose, that a living body is made up of thousands of cells, both unicellular and multi-cellular?'

'I've heard of it being so,' Helen assented; then she wrinkled her nose in obvious disfavour. 'Matter of fact I've never interested myself in squiggly things or those horrible pictures of tadpoles which belong somewhere inside us.'

'Squiggly things and tadpoles have nothing to do with what I'm talking about. I'm strictly concerned with cells, and nothing else. Now, digest this fact in all seriousness: Every living thing is an organism, which is to say that its various parts co-operate to produce a self-regulating individual. Living beings are comprised of both unicellular and multicellular organisms. Each cell is capable of performing and reproducing the activity of the major body as a whole.'

'Well?' Helen asked. 'How far does that get us?'

Jeffrey sighed. 'Apparently you've missed the point. *Each cell is capable of performing and reproducing the activity of the major body as a whole*. That is to say, if a single cell were removed from your body or mine, that single cell can develop into an identical duplicate of the body from which it came.'

'It could? But how? Why?'

'Because it is a living thing in itself, but instead of being isolated and thus forming an individual unit it is lumped together with myriads of other cells and thus remains one unit amongst thousands. It is like one person in a mob, the whole mob forming some kind of body, be it Governmental, political, criminal, or whatever you like.'

Helen looked about her. After a moment she shrugged. 'Sorry to be a wet blanket, Jeff, but I'm no wiser. Why should a single, unformed thing like a cell be capable of completely reproducing the major body of which it is only a part?'

'For this reason: it is nourished by the same foods and bloodstream as the parent body; it is subject to the same environment and nervous impulses. It is a living thing, in the lowest embryonic state. Consider the mechanism of normal birth. A child would be the exact reproduction of its parent if there were not the factors of heredity to be considered. It is these factors that cause children dissimilar to the parents to be born. Given the possibility of only one parent and no antecedents, that child would be a carbon copy of the parent.

And a child is only aggregated cells. So, isolate one cell from an adult human being and subject it to exactly the same processes as a human being undergoes from birth to maturity, and you get a duplicate!'

Helen stood up.

'I don't like it, Jeff!' Her eyes and voice were both intensely serious. 'It's — it's biology gone mad, or something!'

'Anything but it! I've proved it.'

'Proved it! When?'

'Quite recently, using the inevitable white mouse for a subject. I isolated one unicell from a white mouse and gave it the correct treatment. In seven days there was a second white mouse. Impossible to tell one from the other — until one of them died, which I think was the cellular mouse. Since then I've corrected the error. It got too much radiation at a crucial stage in its development.'

There was a curious, bewildered look in Helen's hazel eyes. She did not quite know why she so feared the thesis that Jeffrey had expounded — but she did, with everything that was in her. As yet she had not realised that her sex was instinctively and violently opposed to anything but the natural law of birth. For Jeffrey there were no such considerations.

'When did this horrible idea occur to you?' she asked, and the sharp note of angry fear in her voice made Jeffrey raise his eyebrows.

'It only seems horrible to you, Helen, because you're so completely unscientific. Stated simply it's the greatest biological discovery of the century! When did I get the idea? Long ago. After all, one can't spend one's life as an organic chemist without noticing certain functions. I base my whole thesis on personal observation, known facts, and the statements of famous biologists of the past.'

'Then why was it left to you to discover this — this bizarre development?'

'No biological scientist has seen fit to remove a cell from a human being and develop it into a duplicate of the parent body. I am simply taking a giant's stride and experimenting with an isolated human cell for the first time.'

Suddenly Helen gripped Jeffrey's arm

tightly. 'Jeff, call me crazy, call me anything you like, but call the whole thing off! You're a sort of modern Frankenstein and don't realise it. And anyway, I thought the medical authorities had put a ban on this sort of human experimentation? Has your experiment been sanctioned?'

Jeffrey threw back his head and laughed heartily. 'Oh come now, Helen. That's ridiculous. Good old Frankenstein dug up bits of corpses and put them all together to make his monster. He had the right idea, I suppose, fictionally speaking. This, though, is based on scientific law, and I'm the first man to try it out.' He lost his smile, and hesitated. 'You're right, though, about the restrictions on human experimentation. But those restrictions only apply to *known* lines of biological research. I am pioneering in an entirely *new* field . . . In any case, I'm not turning back now: I've already got things going.'

Helen lowered her hand slowly. 'That was what you meant, then, by a duplicate of yourself?'

'That was what I meant — and

everything's going nicely. Come and look for yourself.'

Jeffrey turned towards the major bulk of his apparatus, but Helen hung back, shaking her head quickly.

'I'd rather not, Jeff. Messy things like this make me feel sick.'

Instead of being intolerant Jeffrey developed a massive calm.

'There's nothing messy or unpleasant about this, Helen: everything is under perfect control. Look for yourself.'

Deliberately he refrained from doing anything to urge her, then after a moment or two she seemed to pluck up courage and came slowly forward. The instrument beside which Jeffrey was standing resembled an immense transparent cylinder, the base of which seemed to be lined with cotton wool, or some spongy white substance. Within the cylinder there was a faint haze of gases, rendered clearly visible by twin beams passing straight through the cylinder from opposite directions and having their source in two automatic projectors.

'Look carefully,' Jeffrey said quietly.

'After all, Helen, you are in this as much as I am. As my wife you'll share the glory.'

'And the tragedy, Jeff. That's the thought that predominates in my mind.'

'Then forget it. Now, take a look.'

It was some little while before Helen could distinguish anything in the mysterious cylinder, then when she did see the object she started in amazement. There, in the midst of the cotton-wool stuff, lay a minute human figure. Or so it appeared to be. It was more than an inch in length, an infinitesimal doll, salmon pink in colour and motionless. Since it was lying on its face Helen was unable to distinguish the features, but a queer feeling surged through her as she pondered the tiny head with its disorder of dark hair.

'Is it — you?'

'A duplicate of me.' Jeffrey nodded in profound satisfaction. 'Ever see anything so perfect? It began as a unicell of about o-point-o-five millimetres in diameter, which I had to extract electrically. I removed it from my thigh, since that was the easiest part on which to work.'

'Was it painful?'

'Heavens, no! Nothing more painful than the prick of a needle, and not a drop of blood was drawn. Whole process was remote controlled by electricity since the naked eye could not sec what was happening. Remote control and the help of the electron microscope enabled me finally to segregate one unicell from the bunch of cells I'd withdrawn. I couldn't extract just one from myself: that would have called for an exactitude beyond my instruments.'

'Then what did you do?'

'I immediately isolated the cell in this cylinder. Within it are the exact gases that compose our atmosphere, together with the correct atmospheric weight — artificially induced — of fourteen pounds to the square inch. That cell there is completely isolated from those which formerly surrounded it. Yesterday it was just a cell, yet it had within it the nucleus, the cytoplasm, the centrosome, and all the necessary functions, including a reserve food supply which is present in all cells. It also possessed a minute quantity of my blood and all the other fluids that make up my body. The two radiations you see are light and ultra-violet composed in one beam — absolute essentials in that they duplicate the sun's own radiation — and the other one is heat at a thermostatically controlled temperature. You can see what has happened. The cell has already lost its cellular appearance and has assumed the outlines of a living being, the outlines of the major body from which it came. Myself! It is the first human being to be born by scientific cellular process.'

Helen stared at it as though hypnotised. Jeffrey's voice seemed to reach her from a great distance.

'All the necessary provisions have been made for the absorption of carbonic dioxide and the disposal of waste materials. All the necessary nutrients for bodily growth are supplied in liquid form, and assimilated by absorption. I'm surprised, but none the less pleased, at the extremely rapid development. Within seven days this microscopic being will have developed into a full-grown man, biologically and chronologically identical with myself — '

'What!' Helen gasped. 'But surely he will just be a baby at first? Take years to develop, like you or I?'

'No.' Jeffrey's voice held a hint of pride. 'I told you my process is something entirely new — revolutionary! Scientists have of course already created duplicate baby animals, using *conventional* science, and the authorities have banned them from duplicating humans because the process they use is inherently unstable, and therefore dangerous. But I have transcended their clumsy methods, by using an entirely different approach. It makes one wonder about the prodigality of Nature. Reminds me of the sunflower with its face full of seed, each seed a new plant, which in itself — '

'And where,' Helen broke in deliberately, 'is it going to stop?'

'Right here with this one duplicate. That should be enough for anybody.'

'More than enough! I still say the whole thing's dangerous, chiefly because it's directly contrary to natural law. And another thing, how is this achievement — if that is what it is — going to make us a fortune? Who on earth will want a duplicate of you?'

'Of me, nobody. But when this process is generally known, think what it is going to mean! Big business men can send doubles of themselves to finish off deals; heads of State can send a duplicate when there's the chance they might get assassinated. Many folk might even consider them useful as servants. A thousand and one possibilities, all of which means money for me and you, because I'm the only scientist who can do it.'

'In a way,' Helen said slowly, 'that makes the prospect even worse! I hadn't realised that these duplicates will be able to think. And I suppose they will?'

'But of course! They will be as individual as the parent body from which they came, and they'll have the advantage of not being subject to hereditary strains and so forth. For the life of me I can't think why that should make the prospect worse.'

'Only because, being able to think for themselves, they will probably not do as you expect. What happens if they — or it — depending on how many are made — refuse to take orders?'

'There's nothing else they can do. They'll be quite uninitiated into the normal ways of living: everything will have to be taught, just as with a child. That way obedience will he enforced, or so I believe.'

'I see — ' Helen turned slowly away from the case, her face troubled. After a moment or two Jeffrey came over to her.

'Look, Helen, if you have to start fretting over this business for heaven's sake leave it until there's something to fret about! There can't be progress in anything — much less in science — without some kind of uncertainty.'

'No, I suppose not,' Helen admitted quietly. 'Well, let's hope everything turns out all right. Are we ready now to carry on towards home?'

'Uh-huh, might as well. Nothing I can do until the cell is more developed. That was why I was heading homewards when you encountered me.'

Helen did not speak again until they were outside the laboratory and Jeffrey had re-set the time lock; then she said:

'I don't see why you couldn't have told me about all this. I had to find out in the finish.'

'I wanted to surprise you with a duplicate of myself but now that's been forestalled. Anyway, I told you no lies. I simply said I was working overtime.'

Helen said no more. There was nothing useful to be gained by argument, and anyway the die was now cast,

And with each succeeding day the unicellular man grew bigger. In what spare time he had Jeffrey visited the laboratory, kept his records up to date and gazed in increasing wonder on the midget duplicate of himself, which was rapidly developing into an 'adult childhood', if such a term can be used. For, though the unicell man rapidly reached the dimensions of a ten-year-old boy, his entire appearance was that of an adult. And the more he studied the face the less Jeffrey liked it. It was a hard cold, expressionless reflection of his own visage, without the good-humoured smile and introspective eyes.

Helen did not visit the laboratory again; she had already seen quite enough. Neither did she ask any questions concerning the duplicate. Instead her manner had become one of silent, even icy, disapproval. At first Jeffrey resented such an attitude, then feeling that his experiment was even more important than Helen, he also assumed a mood of silence and kept away from home as much as possible.

Back of Helen's mind was the constant urge to do something to stop her husband's experiment. As far as she knew she had no gift for seeing future events, but in this case she found it impossible to rid herself of a sense of deepest foreboding. What exactly she *could* do to upset matters she had no idea — but one evening, nearly a week after she had visited the laboratory, there came a chance for her to somewhat unburden her mind, the recipient of the 'unburdening' being Hal Walsh, frequent caller and one of Jeffrey's closest friends.

'He usually gets home around nine these evenings,' Helen said, leading the way into the lounge. 'If you've no objections to waiting ten minutes or so you ought co be able to catch him. Is it anything important?'

'Not particularly.' Hal Walsh seated himself as Helen settled on the chesterfield. 'In fact nothing more than an effort to pass the time of day. I was passing by and thought I might as well see how things are with you. Everything okay?'

'Fine, fine,' Helen said with a tired smile.

'Correct me if I'm wrong, or do I detect an unconvincing note?' Hal studied Helen seriously. She in her turn surveyed him — a big, roly-poly blond of a man with a much higher intellectual quota than one would have imagined. As a chief laboratory research technician he could not afford to be a fool.

'Matter of fact, Hal, everything is crazy,' Helen sighed, sitting back. 'I wish to heaven it were not.'

'Oh? Don't tell me there's a rift in the

domestic lute. I always got the impression that you and Jeffrey hit it off perfectly together — sort of ideal match that I hope I may make some day.'

'This has nothing to do with our connubial bliss, Hal: it relates to a discovery Jeffrey has made. I think it's unspeakably dangerous, but I can't make him see reason. Being the good and trusted friend you are, I think I ought to tell you all about it.'

'I think so, too.' Hal gave his friendly grin. 'Jeffrey always was one for thinking up queer scientific ideas. What's he done this time?'

'Created a human being identical to himself. I don't quite understand it. Something to do with cellular enlargement.'

'You pulling my leg?' Hal's stare was somewhat blank.

'It's as true as I'm sitting here.' And Helen went into the details. When she had concluded she gave a sigh. 'And the whole business has produced a sort of stalemate between Jeffrey and myself. I want him to give up this mad biological experiment, and he just won't see any justification for doing so.'

'I don't blame him,' Hal said, musing, and Helen gave him a hurt look.

'So you're on his side, too? Serves me right for explaining to a man. I've arrived at the conclusion that a man just isn't temperamentally fitted to see how serious a business this is.'

'Serious or otherwise it's an enormous stride forward in biological research. If Jeffrey can pull this thing off in the way he believes he's going to be world famous. Doesn't that compensate you?'

'No. I think he ought to leave Nature to do her own work and not interfere. Anyway, here he is now — ' Helen broke off as there was the sound of a key in the front door. 'He'll be able to tell you everything himself.'

In another moment Jeffrey had come into the room. His somewhat morose expression lightened as he saw Hal Walsh rising to his feet.

'Hello, Hal — quite a time since you breezed in. How's tricks?'

'Fair enough with me.' Hal shook

hands warmly. 'All the fun seems to be on your side, from what I hear.'

'Hear?' Jeffrey gave Helen a startled look, which she met with complete equanimity.

'I've been telling Hal about your duplicate man, Jeffrey, and — '

'Then you had no damned right!' Jeffrey snapped. 'No right at all! I told you the thing was a secret until I'm ready to proclaim the details to the world.'

'But not a secret from *me*, surely?' Hal looked astonished. 'I'm one of your closest friends — '

'I know that, Hal, but — Oh, damn!' Jeffrey sat down irritably. 'Just shows — never trust a woman! Haven't the vaguest idea when to keep their mouth shut!'

'If that's the way you feel about it, all right!' Helen jumped angrily to her feet. 'Frankly, Jeffrey, I'm sick and tired of having this beastly duplicate of yours coming between us, and what is more I — '

'Peace, my children, peace,' Hal murmured, waving his hands soothingly. 'Let

Uncle Hal try and even things up a bit. You both think you're right. Okay, let it go at that. Take my advice, Helen, and don't be too eager to throw the chance of a lifetime overboard. You can't have a fortune without some friction, you know.'

'I'm sorry,' Jeffrey apologised quietly, getting to his feet and putting an arm about Helen's shoulders. 'I didn't mean to bite your head off. I'm edgy, that's what it is. Scared stiff something might go wrong with the duplicate.'

'No such luck, I'm afraid,' Helen sighed, somewhat mollified.

'There you go again! Now look here, Helen — '

'Quiet!' Hal interrupted. 'Sit down the pair of you. Good! Now let's get some sense into this. Tell me exactly what you've done, Jeffrey, and I'll act as a sort of umpire and try and decide whether you've started something dangerous or not. As a research scientist with a fair reputation I ought to be a good judge.'

Jeffrey hesitated, but finally complied, giving all the details that were asked for.

Indeed it only dawned upon him just how much he *had* given away when he came to finish. Not that it mattered, though. He could trust bluff, good-natured Hal.

'Mmm,' Hal said finally, frowning and thinking. 'No doubt about the biological brilliance of the conception, but as to the outcome — Well, I just can't predict anything!'

'There you are!' Helen exclaimed triumphantly. '*Anything* can happen, and that's what I'm worried about.'

'I didn't mean it in that sense.' Hal glanced at her. 'I think from the financial point of view that you and Jeffrey should make a packet. All the big shots will be after a duplicate of themselves for professional reasons. It's just how a duplicate man may react which puzzles me. His own individuality will be something to reckon with — How far has he developed, Jeffrey?'

'Practically to maximum, and that is what is worrying me at the moment. I'd got the idea that he'd have to be taught everything — same as you educate a child. Only he doesn't need it.'

'You'd better explain further,' Hal said, his eyes intent.

'Well, today I had him out of the case for the first time. However, instead of waiting for me to tell him something he told me point blank that he was quite capable of looking after himself!'

'In so many words?' Helen gasped.

'Yes. Perfect English, even though it sounded a bit studied. How in the world he learned to speak it is beyond me.'

'Then it shouldn't be,' Hal said seriously. 'This duplicate man of yours is shorn of all hereditary tendencies and therefore is apart from all the natural laws attendant upon a normally evolving creature. He has taken all his characteristics from you since he is a part of you — a single cell. If a single cell has within itself all the *physical* attributes of the parent body, why shouldn't it have the mental?'

Jeffrey was silent, but it was obvious the idea had come to him as a considerable shock.

'The mentality of an individual is as complete as the physical,' Hal continued. 'The possibility is, therefore, that your duplicate man knows everything that you know because his mind has developed to the same point as your own.'

'That could explain it,' Jerry admitted. 'Certainly he seemed to know everything about me, about my work, what I had done to create him, all about Helen — '

'What!' Helen exclaimed, startled.

'If Hal's theory is right that's only to be expected,' Jeffrey explained.

'And where does your enterprising duplicate go from here?' Hal demanded, his big face grim. 'If his mind development is now equal with yours, before he's even started to think for himself, what happens next? He'll have no restraints. He might not even know the difference between good and bad because those two instincts are born of heredity. He's an absolute outsider.'

'I left him in the laboratory,' Jeffrey said, after thinking for a moment or two. 'He gave me his word that he would not venture out into the world until I had made the necessary provision for him to do so.'

'Then I think you were a sucker to

believe him!' Hal snapped. 'Let's get over there right away and see what's going on. Since I'm in on this as well I might just as well know where things are leading. Feel like coming, Helen?'

She shook her head. 'Not for me, thank you! You know already how I feel!'

2

Jeffrey 2

When Jeffrey and Hal entered the laboratory and switched on the lights they found the duplicate man reclining in a nearby chair. He was fully dressed in the suit which Jeffrey had provided and, judging from the difficulty he seemed to have in seeing the bright light, had probably either been asleep or had his eyes closed in thought.

Silent, Hal weighed up the situation, his eyes moving from Jeffrey to the duplicate. There was not the slightest doubt that one was the absolute 'carbon copy' of the other.

'I call him Jeffrey,' Jeffrey murmured. 'Might as well since he's basically me.'

'Basically, yes,' the duplicate man agreed, rising to his feet. 'But there the affinity ends, I think. Who is this you have brought to see me?'

Hal noticed immediately the studied effort the man made in speaking, as though he were recollecting every word before uttering it. The sharpness of his voice could not be overlooked either: he gave the impression of treating Jeffrey himself as somebody most inferior.

'This is a very good friend of mine — Hal Walsh,' Jeffrey explained. 'Since he knows all the details concerning you — and also because he's a research scientist — I thought he should see you.'

'I see. Exhibition of the specimen, so to speak?'

'In a way,' Jeffrey admitted dubiously.

The cold eyes moved from Jeffrey's face to Hal Walsh's. Hal absorbed the relentless scrutiny without flinching, chiefly because he was a deeply interested man.

'There's no doubt of one thing, Jeff, you've really got something here,' he murmured. 'All depends how the situation is handled.'

'I think,' the duplicate man said, 'that I am better fitted than either of you to make the decisions. You see, I am not limited to being just one man.'

'You're not?' Jeffrey looked surprised. 'But you must be. You are simply a vastly expanded living cell, and therefore — '

'Quite so, but you evolved me — if I may use that term — from a unicell, and if you know your biology correctly you will recall that the unicell multiplies by the simple process of fission.'

'Of course I know!' Jeffrey looked impatient. 'But that does not apply to you.'

'Why doesn't it? I am a single cell, even though expanded to human proportions. Though my physical appearance duplicates yours there is the one difference that I am not made up of tens of thousands of individual cells — as you are — but of one alone, that one containing all the necessary organs which you yourself possess. The difference with me is that, physically speaking, I would be pronounced neuter. More correctly, however, I am asexual and can reproduce myself just as the normal cell does.'

'This is getting out of hand,' Hal muttered. 'You overlooked that the unicell divides by fission to produce two. And that kind of division can go on indefinitely. There could even be tens of thousands of Jeffrey Dexters!'

'Exactly,' the duplicate man agreed as Jeffrey himself wrestled with this monstrous thought. 'And what is more to the point, there will be! You do not imagine that, having conferred an individual existence upon me, I intend to let it stay at that, do you? You do not think I propose to remain your slave, to do as you wish and become the target for inquisitive scientists? No, my plans are much wider in scope than that.'

'What do you intend doing?' Jeffrey demanded. 'I have the right to know!'

When the duplicate man answered there was no change of tone in his voice; no smile, no anything that suggested a human emotion. He was plainly quite devoid of those idiosyncrasies that derive from an ordinary human being's heredity.

'My plans cover a very wide field. One fact is certain: those who shall come after me, and who will inevitably be duplicates of myself and you, will be controlled by me because I am the original. And, further, I have the controlling mind. As to what I intend to do — I fancy you will discover soon enough. First, though, behold what an error you made in assessing me.'

Jeffrey and Hal stood and watched too absorbed to speak as the duplicate man seemed to become slowly transparent, even though his clothes remained solid enough. Before the transparency could become absolute, however, there seemed to step from him a ghost of himself; naked, looking exactly like a dreamer rising from a body in a film sequence.

'The duplicate of the duplicate,' the second Jeffrey explained, his voice still toneless. 'And that reproduction is simply the fission of a giant cell and can be performed as many times as I wish — and each cell those reproduced also has the power to reproduce. The rest is purely a matter of mathematics.'

'A multi-man,' Jeffrey whispered, fascinated. 'That's what I have brought being — one pattern capable of endless reproductions. Ghostly images of the original — '

'But not ghostly for long,' the double interrupted him. 'The semi-transparency of each of us is caused by the drop in energy at the instant of fission. As energy returns so does solidity.'

Which proved to be correct, for in perhaps three minutes both men — the one naked and the other clothed — were apparently firm and solid. The newly-created man did not speak: he seemed rather to be held by the mental influence of his fantastic creator, the original cell.

'Having demonstrated that multiplication is the easiest possible thing, our destiny lies elsewhere,' the duplicate man said. 'Your biological experiment has proven amazingly successful, Jeffrey Dexter. You are to be congratulated.'

'There's still time to stop this,' Hal breathed in Jeffrey's car. 'Kill the pair of them off — now! Stop them getting out!'

'I would advise you not to waste your time,' the duplicate man said, his hearing evidently uncannily acute.

'Being aware of your intentions we would instantly retaliate — '

'It's worth a try, anyhow,' Jeffrey

retorted, and whirled across to the nearby bench. From it he snatched up one of the cases of surgical instruments, which he had used in the experiment, and in a matter of seconds had pulled out a long, viciously keen knife. At the same moment Hal hurled himself forward and thus blocked the sudden advance of the duplicate men, for it was obvious that the 'new' man was automatically obeying the movements, or else the mental commands, of his parent.

'I can create, but I can also destroy,' Jeffrey snapped, wheeling round with the knife in his hand. 'And this isn't murder, either — merely the destruction of an experiment.'

Recklessly he drove the knife blade forward, straight for the duplicate man's heart. He was a fraction too slow, however. Abruptly snatching himself free of Hal's retaining grip the duplicate man slammed out his right fist with a power that was more than human. It struck Jeffrey on the side of the jaw, and the universe blasted outwards in stars.

When he could get a grip on himself

again he found he was slumped in the laboratory chair with Hal bending over him.

'That's better,' Hal muttered, setting aside a jar of sal volatile. 'That devil sure packs the hell of a wallop.'

Jeffrey stirred and then felt his throbbing jaw tenderly.

As he did so he looked about him.

'What happened to those two?' he demanded at length. 'Did you finish them off?'

'You trying to be funny?' Hal asked. 'I wasn't going to risk my life trying to stop them: they're too strong, both of them. Much stronger than ordinary human beings. Besides, I had my hands full getting you straight again. The naked one pretty well stripped you, and there wasn't a thing I could do about it. Then they both left — and that was that.'

'Stripped me?' Jeffrey looked down at himself, realising now that his only clothing consisted of a laboratory overall belted in round the waist. His shoes, socks, collar, tie — every article of clothing had vanished.

'Which leaves the heavenly twins wandering around somewhere in the summer evening,' Hal sighed as he saw that Jeffrey's strength had about returned. 'It even begins to look as though Helen had the right idea when she felt you'd taken on too much.'

'I've enough to worry about without you starting an 'I told you so' routine!'

'Sorry — ' Hal picked up the knife from the floor and looked at it pensively. Jeffrey looked too and then frowned.

'I suppose I'm lucky they didn't use that on me — or did you stop them?'

'I didn't do a thing: I just didn't dare. No thought of murdering you seemed to occur to them, probably because that is a violent emotion begotten of heredity. They only attacked you, I believe, because the instinct of self-preservation made them do it in order to save themselves. Self-preservation isn't an emotion of heredity: it's an individual reaction, which every living creature possesses. In that, therefore, we natural humans are more sadistic because the urge to murder probably occurs to the best of us sometimes.'

'What are you trying to do?' Jeffrey demanded. 'Hold a brief for those two blasted monsters?'

'You know me better than that.' Hal put the knife back in the instrument case and reflected. 'We're right up against it, Jeff, and no mistake.'

'We? This is my particular headache. You don't need lo have any part of it, unless you want to.'

'I'm your friend, aren't I? I consider myself automatically enlisted. The trouble we're up against is massive. Those two can become four at any moment; four can become eight. There's no limit to it once this fission business starts. The devil of it is that you never thought of that angle when using a single cell for your experiment. If only somebody had worked with you — me, for instance. I might have seen the possibility.'

'Useless observations now,' Jeffrey said, getting to his feet and wincing at the cold of the stone floor. 'Best thing to do now is get some clothes. Maybe you wouldn't mind nipping back home and telling Helen to give you a set?'

'Okay.' Hal swung towards the laboratory door and then paused. 'But wait a minute. What's Helen going to think of that? We don't want to advertise, even to her, that two duplicates of yourself are wandering free and unmolested. She might panic. We've got to think carefully what our next move must be.'

'Right enough,' Jeffrey admitted, perching on the bench so he could keep his feet off the floor. 'Tell her I spilt some acid over myself, but that I'm not burned in any way. That ought to do it.'

Hal nodded, opened the door and went on his way.

Jeffrey sat thinking for a while, utterly perplexed by the weird problem confronting him; then after a while there came a hammering on the door. Evidently Hal had forgotten something and of course he did not know how to operate the time-lock. The only solution was for Jeffrey to open the door himself from the inside.

He skipped across the cold stone floor, turned the catch — and then fell back quickly. The first duplicate was outside, standing against the western twilight that divided the two buildings opposite.

In another moment the duplicate was in the laboratory, the door closed, his cold eyes surveying Jeffrey as he retreated slowly towards the bench.

'I have been considering this situation very carefully,' the duplicate said, coming forward. 'It occurs to me that it might be unexpectedly difficult to make a start in society when I am an exact counterpart of yourself. There might be a lot of inquiry, which would hinder my plans. As to the duplicate of myself: I can keep him out of sight until such time as I wish him to appear in public. He is completely under my control.'

'Which means what?' Jeffrey asked curtly.

'It means,' his double replied without emotion, 'that I may as well step into the niche in society which you already occupy. That you are an organic chemist and a respectable member of the community makes you a convenient springboard for my endeavours.'

Jeffrey felt behind him towards the

instrument case. He knew exactly what was coming. It flashed through his mind that his duplicate had probably been waiting for a chance like this — a moment when Hal Walsh would be absent.

Then he whipped the knife out of the case and stood with it ready for action.

'I had the impression,' he said deliberately, 'that the idea of murder would not occur to you. You should not be capable of human emotions — '

'Nor am I. I have no sense of either hatred or affection, much less of murder. I simply see in you a useful means of developing my plans. I can only accomplish my purpose by stepping into your shoes — and that means, of course, that you must he eliminated. That is not murder; it is logic.'

Jeffrey did not wait any longer. He catapulted himself forward from the bench, the knife ready for action.

With superlative ease the duplicate man stepped aside, but at the same instant he whipped up his left hand. It struck Jeffrey's knife forearm with the impact of a steel bar.

Hurtling rapidly forward as he was, the sudden jolt had a tragic result. His arm twisted under the blow and the blade drove straight into his chest. His fall to the concrete finished it, his knife hand beneath him.

Yet when Hal Walsh arrived back with the clothes — and had the door opened for him from the inside — he beheld Jeffrey apparently unchanged, the overall about his otherwise naked form.

'Helen's a bit bothered about you,' Hal said, setting the clothes out, 'Took a bit of doing to explain how you could ruin your clothes with acid and yet not get burned yourself.'

'I suppose so,' the duplicate man said — for he had no idea why Hal had departed.

Hal hesitated, frowning slightly. 'Anything the matter? You sound bad tempered, or sharp, or something. Not often your voice is so brittle.'

'Not often I have so much on my mind.'

Deliberately Jeffrey 2 removed the

overall and began to dress. Hal looked about him, puzzled.

'Queer sort of smell in here — acrid odour. Like fumes of some kind. I'd say nitric acid.'

'It's coming from the adjoining room in there. I passed the time making a few tests and didn't draw the acid off.'

'Oh, I see — ' But just the same Hal did not. He prowled around, looking at this and that, glancing back ever and again towards Jeffrey 2 as he continued dressing. When it came to the point of fixing the collar and tie, which demanded attention to himself in the mirror, Hal seized the opportunity to slip into the small adjoining chamber which was usually used as a dark room. Immediately he switched the light on his eyes travelled to the big full-sized nickel-plated bath against the further wall. It was nearly full of a pellucid fluid and nearby lay half a dozen empty carboys.

'What the devil — ' Hal gazed around him, yet saw nothing to confirm the smouldering suspicion in his mind. 'No, it just couldn't be!'

'What couldn't?' Jeffrey 2 was in the doorway, looking in on him.

'Nothing,' Hal said, shrugging and trying to sound calm. 'I just had a thought.'

'Concerning Jeffrey Dexter perhaps?' his double suggested calmly.

Hal's muscles tightened as he stared at the inscrutable being in the doorway.

'Exactly. Unfortunate for you in many ways that you tumbled to that fact because, of course, I cannot possibly allow you to let the truth be known. I have certain plans and I mean to carry them out. I shall be able to move faster than I thought, thanks to you leaving Jeffrey Dexter alone for a while. I had hoped the deception would not occur to you. Manifestly I was wrong.'

'You killed him — and disposed of the body — in this?' Hal motioned to the bath behind him.

'Precisely. I hadn't the time to empty the bath before I heard your car returning. Perhaps,' the duplicate finished calmly, 'it is just as well. There would appear to be a further use for the acid!'

Hal moved slowly, his big body tensed for a sudden spring — and with sudden abruptness he made it. Instead of catching the duplicate man unawares, however, he received a blow on the side of the head that flattened him to the floor.

'Perhaps,' the duplicate said, 'you haven't yet grasped the fact that I am a perfectly coordinated living being — by which I mean that my muscles respond instantly to the prompting of my brain and react with tremendous violence. It is that which gives me both unerring strength and sense of direction. You cannot possibly get the better of me in physical combat.'

Hal knew it full well, but it was not in him to accept defeat thus easily. He remained where he was on the floor, re-gathering his strength and watching for an opportunity.

'I had the feeling that a situation like this might arise,' the duplicate continued, standing over him. 'Therefore I — '

'Kill me and you'll be arrested for murder!' Hal panted. 'Nothing can prevent that. All your physical strength and mental agility won't stop Scotland Yard getting you.'

Jeffrey 2 continued speaking as though he had never been interrupted.

' — Therefore I made arrangements to cover the very contingency you mention. I can never be arrested for murder because at this moment my exact double, even to the fingerprints, and wearing the clothes of the late Jeffrey Dexter, is in one of the most famous restaurants in town. His purpose is to let it be known that he *is* there. How then could he be here as well?'

'And what,' Hal asked slowly, 'is he using for money?'

'Jeffrey Dexter's money, obviously. There was a fair amount in his wallet. Just a matter of organisation, intended in the first place to cover any difficult moments which may arise if the disappearance of the real Jeffrey Dexter is noticed — but now it can also cover your disappearance as well.'

Hal struggled slowly to his feet, watched narrowly. He had nothing left to save himself except his physical strength, which against any ordinary man would probably have given him the ascendancy — but not against this unicellular man with the perfectly coordinated mind and muscles.

Ten minutes later the duplicate man quietly left the laboratory and set the time-lock on the door. Knowing already the address of Jeffrey's home — which had been printed on his wallet — it did not take him overlong to reach there in Hal's car. Having in his mind an almost carbon copy of everything which had been in Jeffrey's own brain, the matter of driving the car presented but little difficulty.

It was just after midnight when he rang the doorbell. The light came up in the hall, and in another moment Helen was opening the front door.

'No key?' she asked in surprise.

'No key,' Jeffrey 2 confirmed, stepping into the hall.

'When my other suit got ruined with acid I destroyed it — with a complete acid bath. I forgot the keys were in the jacket pocket, and they went as well.'

'I see.' Helen looked out into the summer night.

'Hal's car? Where is he?'

'I dropped him at his house and used the car to come on here more rapidly. I was afraid you'd be wondering I where I'd got to.'

Helen shut the door and looked at Jeffrey 2 in the sombre hall light. A brief, puzzled frown crossed her features.

'First time you've ever done anything to try and alleviate anxiety on my part! What brought it on?'

'Since that's your reaction we may as well drop the subject. Anything prepared for supper?'

'I put up a few sandwiches and the tea won't take a moment.'

Jeffrey 2 nodded and strolled into the louuge whilst Helen hurried towards the kitchen. When she returned with the sandwiches she found 'Jeffrey' seated in the armchair, pondering. He did not appear to have heard her entrance, or if he had he showed no sign of it. In point of fact he was orientating himself to the surroundings. His only foreknowledge of them was from Jeffrey's own conception.

'Here it is,' Helen said rather coldly, and at that Jeffrey 2 gave a start.

'Thanks.' He reached out and took a sandwich, then the cup of tea that was handed to him. Helen helped herself, and after a moment settled on the Chesterfield opposite him.

'Well? What had Hal to say about the double?'

'He didn't tell you anything, then, when he came back for these clothes?'

'He hadn't time. I gave him the things you wanted and he just raced off again. I can't think why he didn't come in now and have a little supper with us.'

Jeffrey 2 shrugged. 'He didn't, and that's all there is to be said about it. As to his reactions about the duplicate — He seemed quite impressed.'

'Which makes you extremely self-satisfied about what you have done, I suppose?'

'I would call the whole thing a masterpiece of biological research.'

'Know something?' Helen asked after a pause.

'Well?' Jeffrey 2 took another sandwich.

'You've been living so closely with this infernal — and I *mean* infernal — duplicate of yours you've even started to talk the same way. At least as I *suppose* he talks — in studied, unnaturally precise English. Sounds quite queer.'

'A mode of speech is something which influences one quicker than anything,' Jeffrey 2 responded calmly. 'There is ample evidence of that when a normally well-spoken person spends many years with uneducated people. Either he becomes slovenly in diction, or they vastly improve. Either way the influence is clearly marked.'

Helen became silent and the little lines of worry returned to her forehead. Jeffrey 2 surveyed her impartially and then went on with his sandwich. There was something decidedly wrong here, and Helen knew it full well. Struck with a sudden thought she got to her feet, deliberately caught her foot in the rug and lunged forward so that she hit the table and sent the sandwiches flying.

Jeffrey 2's reaction was dead negative.

He gazed m surprise, or something that resembled it, then he got to his feet as she straightened up.

'Rather clumsy of you, wasn't it?' he inquired.

Helen backed away, her eyes wide. 'Don't come near me! Don't even *speak* to me! You're *not Jeffrey*!'

The duplicate raised his teacup and finished his drink. Helen still watched him fixedly.

'I fell over that rug on purpose. It also wasn't an accident that I sent the sandwiches flying. Jeffrey would have laughed his head off at a thing like that: he had the most queer sense of humour and his laughter was overpowering. But you — You don't laugh! You don't smile! You never move a muscle!'

Helen's voice finished on a high note that was almost hysteria; then she forced herself to be calm. The duplicate man looked at her steadily, then:

'You have been nearly as quick as Hal Walsh at detecting the truth. I suppose one can expect little else from those intimate with your late husband.'

Helen started, then in spite of herself she came forward.

'Did — did you say my *late* husband?'

'Yes.'

'But what have you done to him? Good God, you don't mean you've murdered him?'

'I believe,' Jeffrey 2 said, musing, 'you would call it that. To me it represents a process of elimination.'

'And Hal Walsh?' Helen's eyes were wide in horror. 'You've killed him too! Of course you have! That's why you came back alone in his car — '

Helen did not wait to say any more. Her emotions completely spilled over and, swinging round, she raced for the door of the lounge. With one lithe bound Jeffrey 2 was there before her.

'You are not leaving here, Helen,' he said flatly.

'You don't imagine I'm going to stay here locked up with you, do you? A monstrous, murdering imitation of my husband! Get away from that door!'

Helen did not quite know where she got her courage from, but she lunged forward and seized the duplicate's arm, using all her strength to try and drag him to one side. Her effort ended in her being flung across the room to finally collapse on the floor beside the Chesterfield. Jeffrey 2 looked down on her then came slowly forward.

'There are one or two facts you should get clear in this extraordinary situation, Helen. Firstly, I have no animosity towards you because emotional reactions are not part of my makeup. By the same token you cannot attract me because I am physically asexual — or more clearly, both sexes in one. You do not appear to stand in the way of the logical development of my plans, therefore you have nothing to fear.'

'Nothing to fear!' Helen laughed huskily. 'And you say you have no emotions! You've got a sense of humour and don't know it!'

Jeffrey 2 looked at her stonily. 'I eliminated your husband and Hal Walsh because they were dangerous to me. You are not, unless you become careless and talk too much. As things stand there is nothing to prevent you living as you have always done and accepting me as your husband. Indeed I demand that in order that my plan can be developed.'

Very slowly Helen got to her feet and then backed away until the bulk of the table prevented her retreating further. Jeffrey 2 did not follow her up. He merely stood and watched her intently.

'And you really think,' she demanded, 'that I shall stay here quiet as a mouse and not tell a soul that you've murdered my husband and Hal Walsh?'

'Yes, I really think so. Unless, of course, you wish to go the same way as them. It is for you to choose — cooperation and comparative freedom, or — '

For a long time Helen was silent. She knew very little about the workings of this duplicate of her husband, and indeed was only just recovering from the stunning shock of realising that he was here confronting her and that her own husband was dead — but of one thing she was reasonably convinced, and that was that he could not read thoughts. Therefore, only one thing mattered to her from here on: she must find a way of exacting revenge for what had happened and get this monstrous travesty of Nature eliminated from the scheme of things.

'Very well,' she said at length, standing erect beside the table, 'I'll cooperate. What do you wish me to do?'

'I have already answered that. Behave exactly as you have always done, accepting me as your husband.'

'And of what use will that be to the furtherance of your plan?'

'Every use. I have no intention of revealing to you what the nature of the plan is since that could easily defeat its own ends. The simple fact is that I can make an easier start as an accepted citizen with a certain position in life.'

'And you think you can pick everything up just where my husband left off?'

'I am convinced of it. Everything your husband knew I know also — and a good deal more besides.'

Helen looked into the unemotional, implacable eyes and could not be sure what she read there. All she realized was that there was a deep, cold feeling inside her. This inscrutable being who never smiled, who knew no emotions, was her captor, and nothing short of the most breakneck strategy would enable her to escape him. Finally she shrugged.

'It's getting very late, and in spite of everything I must try and get some rest. Do as you will. Except for my own room the house is yours.'

'I imagine that your husband and yourself shared the room of which you speak, Helen — but that is something I shall not enforce. I can easily rest down here. I would caution you, however, not to try and escape from your room or use the telephone.'

'If I did,' Helen asked from the door, 'what would you do?'

'Kill you.'

3

Framed for murder

Helen knew better than to ignore the bogus Jeffrey's warning, and not once did she step out of line. The following morning, after a night in which she hardly slept a wink — but which had at least given her a chance to think more clearly — she came down for breakfast to find Jeffrey 2 in the lounge, looking exactly like her husband and yet, in an indefinable way, utterly unlike him.

'I have decided,' he said, when Helen had put breakfast on the table, 'to carry on your husband's occupation without an interruption, commencing as from this morning. The matter of money naturally arises, but I see now how that can be overcome.'

'How?' Helen snapped.

'I shall draw money from his bank. My signature and his are identical. I checked that during the night with various signed papers of his in the bureau there.'

Helen shrugged. No use her making an argument. No use her doing anything except put up with this preposterous situation.

'What I said last night concerning any false moves on your part still goes,' Jeffrey 2 added when the almost silent breakfast had been completed. 'I shall return here at the same hour as your husband used to — eliminating the evenings he spent in his laboratory, that is — and I shall expect to find you here. You have no need to leave the house: whatever you need can be done over the phone.'

'Very well,' Helen answered, shrugging — and such was the commencement of her enforced imprisonment, which for the sake of her own safety she did not feel she dared break.

But even if she was a virtual prisoner there were those outside who were not — and a man as important as Hal Walsh, head of the City Research Bureau, could not just disappear without trace and leave nobody wondering where he was. Certainly the Committee for the Bureau wondered quite a deal as day followed day and there was no sign or word from Hal. Finally Scotland Yard was informed, and with meticulous care they went to work tracing Hal Walsh's last known movements. Automatically their search ended at the Jeffrey Dexter home, chiefly because a car bearing Hal Walsh's registration number had been seen in the vicinity, and also because Hal Walsh was known to be a good friend of Jeffrey Dexter's.

Accordingly, one bright summer morning about ten days after her 'solitary confinement' had begun, Helen found herself opening the door to two broad-shouldered men in light raincoats who had the indefinable stamp of the Yard about them.

'I am a police inspector, madam,' the tallest and broadest one explained, opening his warrant card. 'Chief-Inspector Grantham.'

'Thank heaven!' Helen muttered; and the two men looked surprised.

'It's unusual for anybody to be gratified by the arrival of the police, madam,' the chief-inspector murmured. 'I was — '

'I need help desperately!' Helen broke in. 'Do come in. please!'

The two men glanced at each other and then followed Helen into the lounge. The chief-inspector motioned to his companion.

'Detective-Sergeant Hanbuy, madam. We have been endeavouring to make contact with your husband at the city laboratories, but apparently he is out of town at the moment on a special assignment concerning poisoned food.'

'Yes — I believe he is.' Helen remembered vaguely that Jeffrey 2 had made some reference to such a task.

'That being so, and as matters are urgent,' the chief-inspector continued, 'we feel that you perhaps can help us. You are, of course, Mrs. Helen Dexter?'

'Yes — yes, but as I was telling you I need somebody to — '

'A moment, if you please!' The chief-inspector held up a broad hand and smiled. 'I am doing the questioning, Mrs.

Dexter. I believe you are acquainted with a gentleman by the name of Harold Walsh?'

'I was.'

'By that do you mean the friendship has terminated?'

'I mean he's dead — murdered! And so is my husband.' Helen paced up and down restlessly. 'I wondered how I could get in touch with the police, but I just didn't dare. This monster who has taken my husband's place would have killed me!'

Grantham looked puzzled. 'I'm at a loss, madam. We are assured by the city laboratories that your husband is very much alive and engaged on — '

'He isn't my husband! That's the point. He's a synthetic *duplicate* of my husband, created by some complicated cellular process, which I can't attempt to explain. He murdered my husband *and* Hal Walsh! Believe me, for heaven's sake! It's absolutely true.'

The chief-inspector's expression slowly changed, and the pencil of the sergeant hovered uncertainly over his notebook.

‘I am not prepared to indulge in the realms of fantasy!’ the chief-inspector snapped finally. ‘Mr. Walsh has disappeared and our inquiry concerns that disappearance. You freely admit that he has been murdered and then expect us to believe that this murder was committed by some kind of monster. *Really*, Mrs. Dexter!’

Helen became silent, confused, her cheeks flushed It was just dawning upon her how impossible the whole thing must sound, and it was more than obvious that the Yard men were not the possessors of vivid imaginations.

‘Perhaps, sir,’ the sergeant suggested, ‘we might turn our attention to Mr. Dexter himself and see what he has to say? This duplicate man business *could* he identical twins.’

‘It’s not a case of twins!’ Helen said impatiently. ‘I said *duplicate*, and I meant it. Even down to the fingerprints.’

The Chief-inspector got to his feet decisively, his face grim.

‘I can only assume, madam, that you take me for a fool! I think I should warn you that playing tricks with the law won’t do you any good — ' He hesitated, pondering. 'Tell me, what was your relationship with Mr. Walsh?'

'Relationship? He was just a good friend. I thought I'd made that clear.'

'Your husband approved of this relationship — or friendship, if you prefer it that way.'

'Why, yes! What has that got to do with my husband and Mr. Walsh being murdered?'

'I am not sure — yet. I am just trying to establish some cogent reason for your extraordinary story about a double. Mr. Walsh disappeared — and you say he was murdered — ten days ago. That would be June tenth. We have established that Mr. Walsh was at his duties as usual on that day, but his movements during the evening are hazy. Can you throw any light on his activities?'

Helen nodded promptly. 'He went to the laboratory with my husband, and neither of them ever came back. Only the duplicate.'

'And during that time what were you doing?'

'I was here. I didn't want to go to the laboratory. I had already seen enough.'

'Can you *prove* that you were here?' the chief-inspector asked, and Helen hesitated.

'Not very easily. Mr. Walsh knew — but that isn't much use now.'

'No,' the chief-inspector conceded coldly, 'it hardly is. Thank you anyway, Mrs. Dexter. We'll be looking in again, I expect.'

Before the men could reach the lounge door Helen had intercepted them.

'What do I have to do to convince you that I am a prisoner in my own home?' she demanded. 'Every word I've told you is true.'

The chief-inspector shrugged. 'I think, madam, that if your need were as desperate as you suggest you'd have found a way by now — especially with a telephone — to make your predicament known. I'm afraid I cannot delay any longer now. Good morning.'

With that he went on his way through the hall to the front door. Helen dumbly watched and then finally closed the door upon them. Just how she stood she had no idea, but she found herself even looking forward in relief to a possible arrest. At least that would take her out of Jeffrey 2's clutches.

Meanwhile the two Yard men had reached their official car. They looked at each other as the sergeant switched on the ignition.

'Well?' the chief-inspector asked, raising an eyebrow, 'what do yon make of that lot?'

'Quite plain enough to my mind, sir. The woman's just plain crazy — and unless I completely miss my guess she knows a good deal more about the murder of Walsh than she's telling.'

'Could be,' the inspector admitted, pondering. 'Certainly it is a line of inquiry we must pursue.'

'Back to the Yard now, sir, or to the laboratory for another look around? We might have missed something in regard to Walsh.'

'We might have, but we didn't. No — back to the Yard.'

And when they arrived back in their

office both men had a surprise. Jeffrey Dexter himself was there, waiting for them. He got to his feet and nodded gravely as they entered.

'I didn't expect this,' the inspector said. 'I assume, from the photograph and details we have about you, that you are Jeffrey Dexter.'

'I am, yes. I arrived back at my place of work sooner than I had expected, and they told me you had been inquiring after me — so I thought I'd better come right away. What appears to be the trouble?'

'On reliable authority,' Grantham said, sitting down, 'I am convinced that one Harold Walsh, a friend of yours and your wife's, has been murdered. It's my job to prove that, and the more help you can give me the better.'

Jeffrey 2 did not resume his seat. He moved about restlessly for a moment and then shrugged.

'Since things have got this far there wouldn't be any point in my holding things back?'

'No point whatever.'

'Very well, then. My wife murdered

Walsh. I suppose I ought to have told the police long ago — the moment she admitted the fact to me, but somehow I couldn't bring myself to it.'

At a table in a corner of the office the sergeant made notes. The inspector raised an eyebrow and studied Jeffrey 2 carefully. Accustomed though he was to assessing character the chief-inspector had to admit to himself that he was beaten here. Here was quite the most expressionless, unemotional man he had ever encountered.

'So your wife admitted the murder to you, did she?'

'She did. She committed it ten days ago. As far as I know she went to my laboratory, which is situated in — '

'We know where it is, Mr. Dexter. Keep on with your story.'

'To the best of my knowledge she was more than fond of Hal Walsh, but he tried to live up to certain principles and did his best to cut her out of his life. On the evening he died he went to my laboratory at my request to switch off an important apparatus to which I could not attend myself. My wife followed him there and murdered him. She used an acid bath to destroy the body.'

'Quite effectually too,' the chief-inspector said. 'However, it seems she overlooked that Mr. Walsh had gold fillings in his teeth. They were left behind in the bath, and our pathological department is now examining them. We didn't know to whom they might belong, but now, thanks to your very frank statement, there seems little doubt. We shall know for certain when the dentist who made the fillings has been contacted.'

Jeffrey 2 was silent, his face not betraying in the least what he was thinking. Since he had no emotions, consternation and fear were foreign to him, but there was certainly no doubt of the fact that he was a trifle unbalanced by the news that part of Hal Walsh had not been dissolved.

'And you believe your wife committed this atrocious crime?' the chief-inspector asked bitterly.

'I know she did. She admitted as much to me.'

'And you, Mr. Dexter? You say Mr. Walsh went to your laboratory to perform an important duty with an instrument. What prevented you doing it yourself?'

'I had a business engagement at the Zenith Restaurant. If you wish to check back on the time you'll find I was there all the evening, and most of the time within sight of the *maitre-d'hotel*. When I arrived home I had the news from my wife and went to the laboratory immediately to see for myself.'

'And then you drove home in Mr. Walsh's car?'

'Exactly.'

There was a long silence. The chief-inspector eyed his own personal notes for a moment, then transferred his attention back to Jeffrey 2.

'I think you should know, Mr. Dexter, that your wife blamed the Walsh business on you. She even went further and suggested that you too had been killed and that you are not Jeffrey Dexter at all but a duplicate of him. Some cellular process or other.'

'My wife,' Jeffrey 2 said, 'has been

behaving rather oddly for some time. She probably thought that, as I am engaged on a cellular experiment, she could transfer blame to me.'

'Mmmm. What do you imagine was her motive in murdering Mr. Walsh?'

'Hatred — purely and simply. He refused to respond to the intimacy which she desired, so she killed him. And has evidently done her best to switch the blame to me.'

'Thank you,' Grantham said presently, 'for being so explicit, Mr. Dexter. It will make our task a good deal easier.'

'And my wife?' Jeffrey 2 asked, picking up his hat and turning to the door.

'I can't give you the answer to that one just yet, sir. You'll soon know.'

Jeffrey 2 nodded and the door closed behind him. The chief-inspector gave a little shudder.

'Something about that fellow that gives me the creeps. Cold as a fish.'

'Yes, sir; I felt the same way. But hardly the monster that Mrs. Dexter suggested. What do we do? Charge her?'

'We'll have to the moment we have

absolute proof about Walsh. Those gold fillings from his teeth are our only hope, otherwise without a body we've no case. Damnable business altogether, and somehow in spite of everything I can't see Mrs. Dexter being fiendish enough to drown a man in acid.'

'There have been cases,' the sergeant mused, 'where some women killers have had the face of a Madonna — '

* * *

Three days later Helen was arrested on a charge of murder and promptly removed into custody. Not that the fact troubled Jeffrey 2 in the least. He had been fully prepared for this, and it meant that his style was now no longer cramped. In the brief time he had occupied the shoes of Jeffrey Dexter he had succeeded in making the world at large believe that he was Jeffrey Dexter, and his only existing double was at the moment well hidden away in the deeper dives of the city.

But Jeffrey 2 had a plan, and now was the time to put it into action, but before he did so he spent many hours reading and studying the notes of Jeffrey Dexter concerning his amazing unicell theory. When at last he had the facts clear in his astonishingly quick mind, the duplicate man went to work. His first move was to make an opportunity, whilst supposedly out on an assignment for the city laboratories, to pay a call on Randolph Chester, one of the biggest industrialists of the time. Chester was plainly surprised by a visit from an unknown organic chemist — unknown, that is, except for the unfavourable publicity in the Press concerning Helen — but none the less he granted the interview.

'A man in your position, Mr. Chester, obviously wields a lot of power,' Jeffrey 2 stated calmly, coming straight to the point as he lounged comfortably in the great man's controlling office.

The tycoon, thin, hard as nails, white-haired, smiled coldly.

'Technically I own half the country and I'm supreme boss of steel, iron and armaments — to say nothing of railways and air corporations. What concern is it of yours Mr. Dexter?'

'Just this: I can double and treble your influence, yet at the same time give you a little relief from the enormous load of responsibility you carry.'

'Sounds interesting in theory: how does it work out in practice?'

'Well, it's like this — ' Jeffrey 2 leaned forward confidentially. 'I am an organic chemist and I have happened upon a scientific method whereby I can divide any living thing into two, the one being an exact duplicate of the other, even to the fingerprints.'

Randolph Chester, by no means a fool in scientific matters, did not smile incredulously. In fact he did not smile at all: he just waited for the next.

'It is a perfectly painless operation. All that is needed is to remove one cell from the body concerned and that, within ten days or so, becomes a full-grown duplicate of the parent body.'

'And what good does that do?'

'Surely it's obvious?' Jeffrey 2 spread his hands. 'The duplicate is your eternal servant because yours is the controlling mind. It lives, acts, behaves, speaks like you, but obeys you implicitly. I am sure you can appreciate the advantage of an idea like that! As to the exact method concerned, I wouldn't be a business man if I divulged it.'

'You stick to it,' Chester said, grinning. 'I wouldn't think much of you if you didn't. Just the same I can't believe you can do as you profess. How about a sample? Any way of doing that?'

'Certainly. Name any living thing and I'll duplicate it in ten days.'

'All right. You can borrow my spaniel. If you make two of him we'll talk further.'

'Providing,' Jeffrey 2 said seriously, 'that you never for a moment reveal what is going on. Indeed you hardly would because secrecy is the main essential of having a double.'

'Both for business and private life, eh?' the tycoon grinned. 'Okay — no word out of me. I'll make arrangements to have the spaniel sent to you this evening — er — to the address on this card?'

'That's it.'

And Randolph Chester was as good as

his word. So was Jeffrey 2, and in five days instead of ten he brought to the office two spaniels. Since all spaniels look more or less alike these two attracted no particular notice en route from Jeffrey 2's laboratory to the industrialist's place of business — but Chester himself, knowing exactly what defects and oddities to look for in his dog, was very soon satisfied that the second dog had the same identifications.

'It's damned incredible!' he declared finally. 'How the hell do you do it?'

'That isn't the point,' Jeffrey 2 countered. 'I have proved that it can be done and you have two dogs instead of one, for which I make no charge whatever. You will find that the duplicate dog, which I have marked with an indelible white cross on its ears, will always keep the other one company, actually so that it can obey its parent body's orders. Actually, though, for perfect safely and to conceal the fact that this kind of duplication can be accomplished I would suggest you have the duplicate dog destroyed.'

'Why? It's a perfectly good dog.'

'Yes — but it differs from the original in one respect. It has two sexes in one, and being an animal it may procreate itself any number of times. You might find yourself saddled with hundreds of dogs, all full grown, in next to no time. It's a biological threat, and you'd do best to crush it.'

'I see. I don't know what the devil you're talking about, but at least I can believe the evidence of my own eyes. Always have. Right! And you can do this to a human being? To me?'

'I can — without pain or fuss.'

'And supposing you did it? Would my double be asexual as well?'

'It would, yes, but it would not procreate itself without your own individual permission, so you've nothing to fear there. Your double will be entirely under your control and yet be able to behave exactly like you when your mind's influence is elsewhere.'

The plan thus outlined by Jeffrey 2 was a modification of the original formula devised by Jeffrey Dexter — for in his own development from the parent body

Jeffrey 2 had quickly developed a will of his own and destroyed his creator. This time, for purposes best known to himself, Jeffrey 2 was going to alter the formula to render the created double entirely 'controllable' by the parent body as long as the parent body lived. After that only one person could control the unicellular man, and that would be the original unicellular man himself, Jeffrey 2. Here was power in the making — immense and dangerous power, and the biggest industrialist in the country was right on the brink.

'I've always been one to take a gamble,' he said at length. 'Have to in my business. All right, I'll risk it. You want a letter of exoneration in case anything goes wrong?'

'Nothing will go wrong and no letter is necessary.'

'And your fee for this amazing stunt?'

'Two hundred thousand pounds.'

'That's the hell of a lot of money!'

'Not for what you're getting. For you to be in two places at once will be invaluable, providing of course that it is not known by anybody that you are in two places at once.'

'You can be sure I won't make a mistake like that: it would ruin the whole thing.'

Jeffrey 2 nodded slowly. As long as the secret was kept all would be well: one mistake, though, and Scotland Yard would prick up their ears. Two identical men? The whole scheme was a long chance but Jeffrey 2 had his plan worked out to perfection. The one way to make sure that two industrialists did not appear simultaneously was to destroy the original, leaving behind the unicellular industrialist who would respond to the will of the master unicellular man himself — Jeffrey 2.

'I'll pay it,' Chester decided finally. 'Never worth while haggling over the price for a job when you can't do it yourself. Where do you want me, and when? Won't take long, will it? I'm a busy man?'

'A matter of perhaps an hour — and ten days later your identical twin will be ready.'

So the deal was made, and thereafter everything went exactly as Jeffrey 2 had planned it should. In the course of removing a cluster of cells from the industrialist, and thanks to the intimacy of association which such a surgical job demanded, Jeffrey was able by casual inquiry to learn all he wanted to know in regard to the industrialist's private life — his movements, the kind of men who watched over him, the extent of his family — everything. Nor did Jeffrey 2 forget anything: his memory was too razor-keen for that.

'I don't know whether what I'm saying now is out of place,' Randolph Chester remarked gruffly, fixing the gold cufflinks back in his sleeves, 'but this business concerning your wife must have worried you a good deal.'

Jeffrey 2 shrugged, poring over the microscope. 'I don't allow things to worry me, Mr. Chester. I couldn't work if I did.'

'I admire your powers of detachment. I don't think *I* could take it so calmly if my wife had been roped in on a charge of murder.'

Jeffrey 2 looked up and said quietly: 'What my wife does is no real concern of mine, Mr. Chester. She has her individual inclinations as I have, and I have no power to influence her. She murdered — and has been arrested. I haven't committed any crime, so I am free. It is as simple as that.'

'And what do you suppose the verdict will be? Gold filling from the teeth of the acid-destroyed corpse is mighty slim stuff for the maximum sentence, you know.'

'I think,' the multi-man said, 'that she will be imprisoned for life.'

'I don't. Always a chariness at convicting women, anyway, and in this case the evidence isn't too convincing. Life sentence perhaps — and that will mean fifteen years or so before you see her again.'

Jeffrey 2 said nothing, but his lips tightened slightly.

Because most of his knowledge had come from Jeffrey Dexter, and also because Jeff had not known much about the law anyway, it had never occurred to Jeffrey 2 that Helen might be free in so short a time. Once released she would be the first to spring if ever the least sign of duplication of individuals or animals was noticed. That meant he would have to move faster than he had intended.

'Well, when do I come next?' the industrialist asked putting on his jacket and then smoothing down his hair. 'Or isn't another call necessary?'

'No, another call is not necessary. Before you go, though, perhaps you would like to see the spot where my wife got rid of Hal Walsh? You've read the details in the papers?'

'I've read them, but I'm not morbid-minded. Besides, I've work to catch up on.'

'It won't take a minute.' Jeffrey 2 was quietly persuasive. 'Only in the next department here. Take a look.'

He opened the adjoining door, and with a shrug the industrialist stepped forward and gazed into the space beyond, particularly at the shining, empty bath. Then it seemed to him that the whole world descended on the back of his head, and he crashed down into black oblivion.

Deliberately, as unhurried as always, Jeffrey 2 laid aside the massive metal bar, which he had wielded with such deadly accuracy and for a moment or two he stood gazing down on the senseless man.

'If it were left to him to be certain that he and his duplicate never appear simultaneously there might have been a slip-up,' he mused. 'That would have cost me everything. Now there can be no mistake. I have the duplicate, the cashed cheque for two hundred thousand, and a complete knowledge of his business and private life. Yes, it's worth the risk — but I've got to speed up the evolution of his double.'

So Jeffrey 2 went to work, only deserting his task to attend to his normal business. Any backsliding here might cause a seed of suspicion to be sown, and this he did not intend to risk at any price. He watched also, as day succeeded day, the hue and cry which was raised as it was found that Randolph Chester had disappeared. Where was he? Why had he not left word as to his destination? If something was not heard from him soon foul play would be suspected and the Yard would have to act.

But just in time, four days after 'creation', the unicellular double of Randolph Chester, wearing the industrialist's suit and duplicating him in every particular, returned to the fold. He blamed everything concerning his 'mysterious disappearance' on to his secretary. He *had* said he was flying abroad on urgent business. However, no matter — he was back and the upset subsided.

So far, so good. The greatest industrialist of the country was nothing less than an absolute pawn in the hands of the unicellular man, to be moved and directed as he chose. Until that time came the double reacted entirely to the knowledge he had inherited from the parent body. Consequently, Randolph Chester No. 2 behaved exactly like the original in his business and private life. Later, when Jeffrey 2 was ready, things would be different.

For the time being Jeffrey 2 was prepared to lie low, still very clearly realising how close he had come to perhaps blowing his plans sky-high; then as the trial of Helen came nearer a new and startling thought occurred to him, another possibility which could wreck everything if he did not somehow circumvent it. The outcome of his thoughts on this occasion took him post-haste to Sir Austin Malvern, Helen's defence counsel.

'Is it possible,' Jeffrey 2 asked, in the cloistered sanctuary of the famous counsel's chambers, 'that all reference to my wife's ridiculous story of a duplicate man be suppressed?'

'Why *should* it be suppressed?' Malvern demanded.

'I feel that it throws her pitiful state of mind into such savage relief. Isn't it enough that she murdered Walsh without bringing in that fantastic side issue?'

The counsel reflected; then, 'You have been quite helpful, Mr. Dexter, in the information you have so far given me in the preparation of your wife's defence — but what you ask now is quite impossible. Indeed, most of my case is based on your wife's story of a duplicate man — on the basis of you yourself being nothing more than a biological double of her husband.'

'But it's fantastic!'

'Certainly it is — and therefore a wonderfully sound reason for securing a commuting of the sentence of life imprisonment. We can probably save her from that on a plea of 'Guilty but insane'. It's the only chance: the prosecution is in a strong position.'

'With only gold fillings to go upon?'

'They don't need any more with witnesses to prove that the gold fillings belonged to the unfortunate Harold Walsh. That, though, is not the matter at issue, Mr. Dexter. You want the story of your wife's fantastic claim suppressed to spare the state of her mind being advertised. I tell you it can't be done because it's the kingpin of the defence.'

'You cannot find any other way?'

'No. And forgive me saying it, but your habitually callous attitude towards your wife so far makes your present desire to shield her seem most irrelevant.'

Jeffrey 2 did not look annoyed. No expression whatever registered on his deadpan face. He got to his feet deliberately.

'I am more than sorry that my wife's mental derangement should have to be dragged into the limelight in order to mitigate the sentence against her.'

The counsel shrugged but did not answer. For a moment Jeffrey 2 looked at him thoughtfully — then he silently left the chambers.

4

March of the duplicates

Having failed on this particular count Jeffrey 2 made no further moves for the time being. He toyed for a while with the idea of 'eliminating' the defence counsel, backed by the thought that a second lawyer might be more amenable to the idea of suppressing Helen's story of a double, then he abandoned the notion. Sir Austin Malvern was a very famous man and his murder at this vital time, however cunningly it might be contrived, would be bound to raise a host of complications. No, better to see how the trial went and how much publicity was given to the 'double' theory.

As things worked out, events played straight into Jeffrey's hands. Sir Austin Malvern had given more heed to his plea than had been apparent at the time. Somehow he managed to have part of the trial proceedings heard in camera, due to the remarkable 'mental delusions' of the accused. Which meant that the Press only reported the bare bones of the trial, and no hint of the 'double' theory leaked out. The verdict came in as 'Guilty, but Insane,' exactly as Sir Austin had hoped.

Jeffrey 2 was satisfied. This meant that for fifteen years or more Helen would be out of the way. It also meant that other potential victims he intended tackling would not he aware of the possibility that he was a double of the original Jeffrey Dexter. Had this theory been suggested, through Helen's story, Jeffrey 2 would have found it impossible to continue his activities without raising dire suspicions.

That he did not visit Helen in prison was taken by the authorities to mean that he was too disgusted with his 'wife' to do so. As for Helen herself, she had completely given up hope and resigned herself to her fate. In the space of a month she had lost her husband and her liberty, so nothing else seemed to matter very much.

Then Jeffrey 2 went into action again

and contacted Alvin Summers, one of the most famous newspaper, television, and movie reporters of the day. Summers was one of those beings who had the key to the public's heart. Whatever he said was believed and acted upon, therefore he was an integral part of Jeffrey 2's scheme.

Alvin Summers showed no hesitation at falling for the idea of a double. It would enable him to lie low and take a much-needed rest whilst his double did most of the work for him. Like Randolph Chester, he demanded a sample before agreeing to being involved in the business. Once he had this he was satisfied — and like Chester before him he suffered the same fate and left behind a most useful duplicate. Nobody was any the wiser and Jeffrey 2 was again financially better off from the agreed fee, though he had deliberately kept this below the high sum demanded of Randolph Chester.

Such was the measure of Jeffrey 2's slow and insidious progress towards his goal, and from his point of view the beauty of it lay in the fact that nobody was aware that murder had been done. To the world it looked just as though Chester and Summers were still carrying on as of yore.

So, one by one, the great ones fell into the trap and were never personally seen again. Their duplicates carried on their work, and would continue to do so until Jeffrey 2 was ready to operate the second part of his scheme — and this did not come until six months after the trial of Helen.

Then, here and there, a determined voice began to be raised in public — and as usual the long-suffering public gave heed.

'Why,' demanded Alvin Summers 2, in a special leader, 'do men and women everywhere continue to tolerate government by men and women who are in a position of authority solely to benefit themselves? The days when a high-up existed to benefit the country at large have gone. This is the age where men and women blindly accept every order which is given — be it a march to war or a raid on their incomes.'

Accepted as written there was nothing

in this leader but apparent propaganda. Tens of thousands of Britishers read it and thought no more about it; but on the other hand several hundreds wondered if it was the beginning of something, if it was perhaps the onset of the great social revolution predicted by students of public affairs for many decades.

Whether it was coincidence or not nobody knew, but at this time Kenneth B. Jenkins, Britain's greatest maker of movie spectacles in three-dimensional colour, produced and released in record time a film purporting to show Britain basking in the benefits conferred by a scientific dictator, instead of enduring the austerity of a normal government. The film was a huge success. It enabled Britain anyway to see itself through rose-coloured spectacles — and indeed it whetted the appetite of the more imaginative and made them wonder if perhaps such a dream might not be made to come true.

Coincidence piled upon coincidence when Andrew Baker, the famous playwright, turned in a masterpiece showing the rise of an ordinary organic chemist to being dictator of the world. This main character was pictured as the acme of benevolence, and wherever the play was performed it made the audience sigh for an interpretation in actual fact.

It seemed that in every walk of life at this stage there was a great inner stirring towards the overthrow of conventional government and the institution of a scientific dictator who would throw outmoded laws overboard and start a new regime altogether. As usual it was left to the great Alvin Summers 2 to sum up this general mood — this time through the medium of a television interview.

'There is no doubt to my mind,' Summers 2 said, in response to the interviewer's questioning, 'that the public today is more than ready for a change. You see it expressed everywhere by those whose task it is to form public opinion. Take my own leader articles, written in all seriousness after a careful analysis of the public pulse; take Kenneth B. Jenkins's cinematic masterpiece or Andrew Baker's great play. Add to that the other big men — Randolph Chester for one — who have declared openly that they would welcome a change of governmental system, and what does it all add up to? Nothing more than the need to nominate a man or woman, according to inclination, who has the ability and the fire to carry the public along a new road.'

'Very interesting,' the interviewer conceded with a nervous pull at his tie. 'And what do you envisage as this new road, Mr. Summers?'

'I am only a reporter,' Summers answered with that complete lack of emotion common to all unicellular doubles. 'I have no claims to greatness, except what I have earned in the literary sphere, and therefore I can speak as an ordinary man. I would suggest the setting up of a scientist — a one like the lowly organic chemist depicted in Baker's play — for it is a world of science we live in today. Politics and the bickering of Party opinions do not in any way help the community to advance, but science does. A scientist would ride over all these silly and trifling issues and set the human race on the road to doing the really great things. The further exploitation of space, for one thing, held up purely because shortsighted governments will not spend the money for this vital purpose. The mastery of the intricacies of nuclear science for another thing. Vast strides in medical research, the development of a hundred and one vital arts. Only a scientist can promote these things if he be in a position of authority — so my considered opinion is that the public should demand — *demand*! — an election and the nomination of a scientist capable of taking the reins of government.'

'Do you know such a man, sir?' the interviewer questioned.

'As a matter of fact I do.' Summers 2 made the admission after a moment's thought. 'I hesitate to mention him because of an unfortunate incident in his domestic life — but since this in no way affects his scientific ability I would perhaps be foolish in not mentioning him.'

'Perhaps you would,' the interviewer admitted gravely. 'Who is this man?'

'By name Jeffrey Dexter, husband of the unfortunate Helen Dexter who was recently sentenced for murder. In the course of my activities I have heard a good deal concerning Jeffrey Dexter, and developed a profound respect for his wide scientific outlook. Professionally he is an organic chemist, but the range of his knowledge, and of society in general, goes far beyond this. Yes, I would unhesitatingly recommend him.'

Jeffrey 2 heard and saw this entire interview and smiled to himself at the superb way in which it had developed.

Summers 2, being completely under his domination, had spoken just as he had intended he should — and this was the commencement of the great demand for Jeffrey Dexter as a nominee for election in a new scientific government.

Automatically, the public divided itself into two schools — scientific and non-scientific, but the latter group stood little chance against the powerful men and women who all spoke with the same voice: Let Jeffrey Dexter become the leader.

At first the existing government looked upon the development in much the same way that a tolerant parent pretends not to notice the experiments of a child — but gradually, as the passing of the weeks brought more and more public demand for a General Election, it became evident that something had to be done. Jeffrey Dexter *had* been nominated: that had not proven difficult, but few pretenders to country dictatorship had, in the past, equaled the terrific campaign put up by this individual. He seemed to be here, there and everywhere, always up to the mark, always having something intelligent to say, and, above all, always convincing. Not that there was anything miraculous about his appearances in widely separated places: he simply employed as many doubles as he wished, all of them under his control and disappearing whenever he wished it.

In captivity, Helen Dexter heard of these upheavals in a remote kind of way, and immediately renewed her passionate declarations that this being who had the mantle of her husband was out to undermine the country. He could not possibly have any intention of conferring benefit, for his lack of emotion prevented any such human feeling. He was only concerned for himself — and what his ultimate plan was could only become apparent when he had reached the authority for which he was striving.

But of course Helen was ignored. She was a condemned woman and reputed to be mentally unbalanced into the bargain. There was certainly nothing to be gained by heeding *her* wildcat statements.

And it was in the midst of this chaos that a singular experience befell Sir Gerald Ransome, the influential president of the Incorporated Society of Master-Scientists. Business had demanded his presence in the northern city of Manchester and he also fell into the midst of one of the largest campaigns Jeffrey 2 had so far launched. Using Manchester Free Trade Hall, the one of several duplicates or Jeffrey 2 spoke earnestly of his intentions if he were elected to power and indeed *if* an election were granted. Sir

Gerald listened to some of the speechifying and then, informed that the meeting would not end for another hour, he went on his way to catch the London-bound train.

His next stop was at Birmingham and, with twenty minutes to kill before the train moved on, he wandered into the refreshment room for a snack. It was as he masticated a ham sandwich that he caught sight of a swiftly-moving figure with a brief case, looking for a table at which to settle. No doubt of one thing: it was Jeffrey Dexter.

'I'll be damned,' Sir Gerald muttered blankly, and then glanced at his watch. Since this did not satisfy him he got to his feet and ambled over to where Jeffrey Dexter had finally settled.

'Mr. Dexter, isn't it?' he asked pleasantly.

'Surely,' the multi-Dexter assented with complete lack of emotion.

'Mind if I sit down?' Sir Gerald did not wait for confirmation: he dropped his well-upholstered form on the nearby chair. 'I wanted to congratulate you on your Manchester campaign — fine piece of oratory.'

'Manchester?' Dexter in multiple looked surprised for a moment — then back to the deadpan again. 'Oh, *Manchester*! Yes, I think I made a deal of headway.'

'Besides moving at lightning speed,' Sir Gerald added. 'You had half an hour to go when I left the Free Trade Hall, yet you must have come in on this train. Same one as I travelled on.'

'Yes. The meeting was cut short.'

'When it was going so well? How surprising!'

Silence. Dexter in multiple resumed the eating of his sandwich, apparently not in the least disturbed. After a moment or two Sir Gerald gave a smile.

'At least Manchester didn't live up to its music hall reputation for once. Not a drop of rain!'

'Not a drop,' Jeffrey multi-Dexter agreed. 'Which helped my audience to swell to capacity.'

Sir Gerald considered his watch once again. 'Train's on the move soon; I've got to be getting back. Care to finish the trip to London with me?'

'I would have done so gladly, only I'm staying here to attend to one or two election details.'

'Good! Best of luck — '

Sir Gerald rose and went on his way, a very thoughtful and certainly much baffled man. When the train got on the move again he did a good deal of thinking. For one thing it was unheard of to cut short a successful political campaign, especially when the hall had been hired specifically for the purpose; and for another Manchester *had* lived up to its tradition, for it had rained non-stop all day. All of which, to Sir Gerald, seemed to add up to the historical observation that there was 'something rotten in the State of Denmark'.

He would probably have felt profoundly moved had he known of Helen Dexter's frequent declarations, only he did not know, for they had never been made public. Nevertheless, he was puzzled enough by the time he arrived in London to check up carefully on the exact time the Manchester meeting had finished. This brought the revelation that it had ended when Sir Gerald's train had been on the outskirts of Derbyshire! That multi-Dexter had taken a plane was possible, only he himself had denied that fact. Which could only mean that there was either more than one Jeffrey Dexter or else he had an exact double who had found some amusement in being mistaken for Britain's greatest campaigner.

The fault lay, of course, with Jeffrey 2. In moving so many of his doubles around the country — or, more correctly, moving so many of his pawns about the political chessboard — he had made the mistake of having two on view at the same time and the always possible coincidence had come off, in that somebody of intelligence had happened to see *both* men.

The man in the street would probably have shrugged the thing off as one of those unexplainable things, but Sir Gerald was a man of authority, influence and purpose. He did not like the idea of a scientific dictator anyway, even though he was a scientist himself: even less did he like a mystery he could not solve. He could contact Jeffrey Dexter's campaign headquarters in London; he could report the riddle to Scotland Yard; or last of all he could explain the business to Arthur Barrington, his closest friend and a member of the Cabinet. And it was this final course upon which he decided.

'You're up against it with this Dexter individual anyway,' he said bluntly, as Barrington listened attentively in the Over Forty Club. 'If there's some jiggery-pokery going on, as I am sure there is, this might be a chance to spike his guns. Of one thing I am convinced: there are *two* Jeffrey Dexters!'

Arthur Barrington did not commit himself in any way: he would not have been a good Cabinet Minister if he had. But in his own mind he was quite convinced that Sir Gerald had got something, and so he immediately started a 'hint and whisper' campaign in the Party's newspapers, bringing it home to the public that their much-favoured future dictator might not be playing the game straight. In other words he was perhaps making use of a twin brother, or somebody very much like himself, to out-manoeuvre the Government representatives.

'Twin brother?' repeated Chief-Inspector Grantham when he saw the news in the morning paper. 'A twin brother of Jeffrey Dexter? He damned well hasn't got a twin brother! We've checked on it. What does, it sound like to you?'

Detective-Sergeant Hanbuy, at his desk in the corner, pondered for a moment or two — then he gave an uneasy glance.

'I don't like saying it, sir, but offhand it sort of looks as though Helen Dexter might have really *meant* that story of hers — '

'Mmmm. Well, she can always be released and compensated if she's proven to be right after all. Definitely there's something queer going on here. Get me Barrington on the phone, will you?'

'Right, sir.'

From Arthur Barrington Chief-Inspector Grantham was referred to Sir Gerald Ransome as the author of the 'double' story — and once he had heard it first hand the chief-inspector moved further, calling on Jeffrey 2 at the city laboratories — and catching him at work instead of being away on an assignment.

'Just a word I'd like with you, Mr. Dexter,' the chief-inspector explained. 'Is there somewhere we can talk privately?'

'Surely. This way.' Jeffrey led the way into a quiet anteroom and closed the door. 'Now, Inspector, what is it? I hardly need to tell you I'm a busy man.'

'I'm aware of it — both as an organic chemist and as a future dictator — you hope. This happens to be vital, though. Have you, in your political activities, employed a double?'

Jeffrey 2 was silent, prevented from embarrassment by his total lack of emotion.

'I thought,' he said finally, 'that we had disposed of that ridiculous theory concerning a double long ago.'

'I thought so too: now it has unexpectedly come up again. I have an unimpeachable witness who says he saw you both in Manchester and Birmingham and that, the timing being as it was, you could not possibly have been in both places.'

'I would suggest that your 'unimpeachable witness' gets his facts straight, Inspector. He says he saw my double: I say that such a thing was frankly impossible. A *resemblance*, maybe, for that could happen to anybody, but not a double.'

'And that,' the chief-inspector asked quietly, 'is all you can tell me?'

'It is.'

So Grantham wasted no more time. He went straight back to Sir Gerald Ransome.

'I am sure, Sir Gerald,' the chief-inspector insisted, when he told of the interview, 'that we're on to something. I'm more than personally interested since I was the one who arrested Mrs. Dexter. If that poor woman was telling the truth after all — '

'The truth?' Sir Gerald repeated. 'To what are you referring? I'm completely in the dark.'

Grantham started. 'Oh, so you are! I'd forgotten that! To cut a long story short, she insisted that Jeffrey Dexter — the present one — is not a normal man at all, but the product of some kind of cellular experiment. You can't blame me for not believing *that*. She insisted that her husband had been murdered along with Hal Walsh, a friend of the family, and this cellular man was responsible. I didn't believe a word of it, but now — '

The chief-inspector's eyes took on a faraway look, and for a while there was a somewhat incredulous silence in Sir Gerald's big office from where he controlled the far-flung destinies of the Incorporated Society of Master-Scientists.

'Fingerprints wouldn't prove anything, either,' Grantham added, becoming alert again. 'They just couldn't if Mrs. Dexter's story of an exact duplicate should be true. And anyway we can't take any fingerprints without some kind of conviction. It's against the Judges' Rules.'

'It certainly does look as though we're in the midst of something very peculiar,' Sir Gerald admitted, musing. 'For the life of me I cannot imagine Mrs. Dexter making a statement like that if it wasn't true. It is so — so *scientific*. A cellular man is possible, you know. Long ago experimental scientists visualised its possibilities, but they went no further. I'm sure no ordinary woman would invent a theory like that if it didn't have a spark of fact in it.'

'I'm left wondering why the devil I didn't come to you in the first place, Sir Gerald,' Grantham muttered. 'Supposing Mrs. Dexter is correct, how do we set about finding the truth? The present Jeffrey Dexter — if fake he be — certainly doesn't intend to betray anything. The point is: could *he* double for *himself*, as he seems to be doing?'

'Very easily. In fact, if the cellular hypothesis were 'given its head', so to speak, there could be any number of duplicates from the original — as many duplicates indeed as there are cells to the body. If the basis should be the unicell, the duplication would take place by fission, which is the normal process.'

Grantham set his jaw. 'Seems to me we've got to act very fast and very thoroughly. If this Dexter fellow is some kind of scientific fluke he might be capable of anything if he can manoeuvre himself into a position of power. I'm a complete novice in scientific matters, but you are not. What's your proposal?'

'All I can do is have Jeffrey Dexter's record at the city laboratories carefully checked — see if there is the remotest clue which might point to him having been engaged on cellular experiments. If so, we might — '

'But of course he was! I know that much. He had a laboratory of his own, small but efficient. That's where the murders took place.'

'Then in that case we can't do better than visit that laboratory and see what it can tell us. There may be a good deal which your uninitiated eye might miss which to me might suggest something significant.'

'I grant you that, but — ' Grantham looked rueful. 'I have no authority to go breaking into Dexter's private laboratory. I lost that privilege once I'd brought the murder business to what I believed was a satisfactory conclusion.'

'Then *I'll* do the breaking-in myself.

You can cither turn a blind eye or arrest me for trespass or something, but information we have got to get! Now, let us discover when Dexter is due at an election meeting: that will assure he is out of the way.'

This information was not difficult to obtain, which meant that at nightfall that evening Grantham and Sir Gerald reached the deserted mid-city ferrocrete laboratory and found themselves confronted with the massive door and its complicated lock. They looked at each other.

'There can't be anything very normal here or there wouldn't be a lock like this,' Sir Gerald decided. 'Looks like one of those time-operated things — and if so it has us beaten.'

'Perhaps we might — ' Chief-Inspector Grantham paused abruptly and it was not usual for his heavy jaw to sag in surprise. But it did now. From somewhere around the rear of the ferrocrete building Jeffrey 2 had made his appearance, neatly dressed, as coldly inscrutable as ever.

'Good evening, gentlemen,' he greeted

politely. 'And I make no apology for surprising you. I expected you would finish up here sooner or later.'

'But — but you are at a meeting at the other side of London!' Grantham exclaimed. 'We watched you on television before we came here.'

'Very ingenious of you — and no more than I would have expected from an unimaginative policeman. But I am surprised that you, Sir Gerald, were so easily led astray. As a scientist you must have guessed the truth by now.'

'I guessed it, yes,' Sir Gerald admitted, 'but I couldn't believe it.'

Jeffrey 2 reflected briefly, then: 'Might I inquire your reason for being so interested in this laboratory?'

'I can explain that quickly enough,' Grantham snapped. 'I have come round lo believing that Mrs. Dexter's story was true, and that you are a duplicate man, different to any other man ever known. In the hope of finding some facts we decided to search this laboratory — Sir Gerald as a scientist and myself as a police officer.'

'Without a search warrant or authority?

Very foolish of you, Inspector. I know my civil rights, even if I am a unicell man. Oh, so that surprises you? I'm merely admitting what you have both already guessed. I feel, though, that since this is the initial stage of your investigation, that you have not yet discussed your theory with anybody else?'

'Not without proof,' the chief-inspector grunted. 'That would be idiotic.'

'I agree. It does, however, make it that only you two men know the real truth. You two men are the only ones who could possibly upset my arrangements. So far I have taken care of all such 'possibilities', and I do not intend to call a halt now.'

The chief-inspector and Sir Gerald glanced at each other sharply — then down at the automatic in Jeffrey 2's hand.

'Believe me, gentlemen, I am in deadly earnest. Remember that you are not dealing with some power-crazy maniac who doesn't stop at murder. You are dealing with a coldly precise scientist whose physical make-up is as apart from yours as anything can be. You do not feel revulsion at the destruction of germs and microbes. I do not feel revulsion when I destroy humans. I remove whatever hinders me. But you wanted to see the laboratory, I gather? You shall.'

Grantham and Sir Gerald made uncertain movements, but they did not dare take action. They knew perfectly well that they were up against something completely inhuman. On the other hand, once they were inside the laboratory —

But there was no time to weigh up the situation.

Jeffrey 2 disengaged the main control of the time-lock, meanwhile keeping his gun trained; then he swung the door open.

'After you, gentlemen.'

There was nothing else for it. Detective and scientist stepped into the cool, roomy area and the door closed behind them, which automatically brought on the lights.

Jeffrey 2 still kept his gun ready, obviously taking no chances.

'I knew you had guessed the trick when you came to see me this morning, Inspector,' he explained. 'The blunder of being in Manchester and Birmingham was entirely mine but since I have narrowed everything down to you and Sir Gerald here I can now take the necessary steps to eradicate the consequences of that blunder. With my campaign in its present advanced stage I must naturally blot out anything liable to terminate it.'

'From all this then,' Sir Gerald said, 'we are to understand that the original Jeffrey Dexter did actually succeed in making the unicellular theory practical?'

'He did — and it was quite a brilliant feat. What he did *not* realise was that he was opening the door to a new race of unicellular men, constantly multiplying upon themselves, a race undeterred by the curses of heredity and with their brains free and unclogged by impure bloodstreams. My plan is to bring about the day of the Unicell Men. They will wipe the normal human beings from the face of the planet. They will be ruled entirely by the *first* uni-cell man — myself. To that end my campaign is directed. Once I achieve the position of dictatorial power, a necessary first step, the rest will follow automatically.'

'You will find considerable opposition,' Sir Gerald declared bitterly.

'I know; and I am prepared for it, but there can be no doubt as to the final outcome. You see, I have the advantage over human beings because I can create what I like *where* I like. From that rather ambiguous statement you may perhaps gather why it is that so many public figures are fighting for my election.'

'You — you mean that Alvin Summers, and the rest of them — ? Those who have been speaking so ardently for you — ?' Sir Gerald stopped, aghast.

'Duplicates,' Jeffrey 2 assented. 'Taking the place of the originals and saying exactly what I wanted them to say. A most useful way of campaigning, believe me. But enough of this conversation, gentlemen. We must have some action. I will grant you the concession of explaining what I intend doing. You are going to be eliminated.'

The chief-inspector gave a grim smile. 'That won't do you much good, my friend. You can't dispose of a well-known

Yard man and a scientist as famous as Sir Gerald without causing a good deal of trouble. The moment our disappearance is noticed we will be searched for and — '

'Your disappearance will *not* be noticed. Do you think I'd be so foolish as that? Before you die you will contribute a single cell each which will automatically ensure my safety.'

Words were no longer any use, and the chief-inspector knew it. Ignoring the gun he suddenly leapt forward and came to grips with the multi-man — but like others before him Grantham soon found he was dealing with a creature of superhuman strength. In a matter of seconds he had been whirled backwards, forced against the bench, and a nauseating odour flooded his nostrils from a heavily soaked pad. Before he could put up any further struggle his senses reeled and he tumbled helplessly to the floor.

Sir Gerald remained where he was, his face pale and set. He knew what was coming; and he also knew that he had got past the age when he could physically cope with his enemy. Almost without resistance he allowed the multi-man to clamp the pad over his face, and for him too the blackness of unconsciousness descended.

5

The Dictator

The members of the Incorporated Society of Master-Scientists certainly noticed Sir Gerald Ransome's mysterious disappearance, but at first inquiry was not too searching. Sir Gerald was a man of many interests and considerable wealth, so it was just possible that he had suddenly departed on business. Even his family, scattered in various places abroad, were not too concerned — yet.

With Chief-Inspector Grantham, though, it was a different matter. Always when he set out on a prolonged mission he left word where he could be reached. For him to virtually disappear was unheard of — and for Detective-Sergeant Hanbuy it was alarming. The last he had heard of his superior was when he had set off to make inquiry of Arthur Barrington — so Hanbuy did not take long in getting the wheels moving to locate the chief-inspector.

Without success. Every effort was made; everybody relative to the problem, which included Jeffrey 2 himself, was closely interrogated, but nothing emerged. Hanbuy even secured the necessary permit to search the Jeffrey Dexter laboratory, and found nothing to confirm his suspicions. Certainly neither he nor his men were scientists enough to attach any importance to as yet improperly formed embryos sealed in a transparent case.

Whom to accuse? Had Sir Gerald Ransome and Grantham really vanished, or were they following some trail together that made it impossible to communicate? Hanbuy did not know what to think, but he went on trying — and Jeffrey 2 for his part made every one of his own moves in complete secrecy. He knew his movements were watched, but he overcame this difficulty by having one of his doubles act for him and so draw the policemen away on an innocuous errand.

Meantime the high-pressure campaign of 'Dexter for Leader' continued, backed by the majority of the newspapers and television circuits. Not all the heads of these organisations were duplicates under Jeffrey 2's direct control, but those who were pulled the others along with them, until at last the Government itself was forced to bow to public opinion and consent to a General Election.

This announcement came ten days after the mysterious disappearance of Sir Gerald Ransome and Chief-Inspector Grantham, and it was also at this time that these two gentlemen returned, apparently quite unconcerned by the sensation they had caused. Sir Gerald returned to his headquarters, and Grantham to his office — the latter walking in during mid-morning and nodding briefly co the astonished Hanbuy.

'What on earth happened, sir?' the detective-sergeant demanded in amazement. 'Where did you vanish to in the last ten days?'

'Oh, that?' Grantham hung up his hat and went across to his desk. 'Matter of fact, Sir Gerald and I got on to a new line and we had to follow it quickly. It took us right to the other side of the world — and there the trail evaporated. Time wasted!'

'Everybody has been wondering what had happened to you and Sir Gerald, sir — everybody from the newspapers to the Assistant Commissioner himself.'

'It's nice to discover I was missed. Just one of those things.'

Hanbuy frowned to himself, a much-puzzled man. There were certain things about his chief that he found hard to reconcile. He knew him intimately, having worked so long beside him, and there were little unexplainable 'differences' for which he could not account. Sense of humour for one thing: yet here was Grantham without a smile or expression. A stickler for regulations too — yet here he was shrugging off a ten-day absence. Odd the way he talked too — sort of clipped and cut short.

'Well?' Grantham asked, gazing steadily, and at that Hanbuy gave a little start.

'Sorry, sir — just trying to place something. Do I understand you to mean, then, that we're no further with the 'twin' business concerning Jeffrey Dexter?'

'Best thing we can do is forget all about that angle. I've found out enough to be sure that the twin business is impossible. Just a lot of newspaper sensationalism — and Sir Gerald will bear me out on that. Far as I'm concerned the Dexter affair is washed up.'

'Yes, sir — if you say so. You'll have noticed he's got his way in demanding an election?'

'I noticed, yes — and come to think of it I'm none too sure but what he mightn't make a difference to things. New brooms sweep clean, you know.'

Hanbuy merely nodded and wandered back to his desk in the corner. He wanted to do a good deal of private thinking, and this move seemed to be the best way to accomplish it.

And as far as Jeffrey 2 himself was concerned he was satisfied that he had stopped up all the leaks likely to upset his arrangements. Only Sir Gerald and the chief-inspector had known the truth, and now their duplicates were in charge and saying only those things which it was dictated to them to say. Thus freed of anxieties from side issues, Jeffrey 2 plunged everything he had got into the final stages of his election campaign.

There was no wonder attached to the fact that he won it. Having so many doubles who could appear wherever and whenever he wanted, the opposition simply could not keep up with him. The result was that he was swept to eminence with a landslide of votes and seventy-five per cent of the country went crazy with jubilation that their hero had been swept to power. There was, in the hysteria that swept through usually staid Britain, something grimly reminiscent of the days before Adolf Hitler's rise to power.

It was when the result of the election was known that Jeffrey 2 was called upon to speak to the massed thousands who had gathered outside his headquarters in the city centre. With his usual unmoved calm he stepped out on the high balcony of his headquarters building and surveyed the floodlit multitude. From various vantage points the telephoto lenses of the television cameras picked up his image and radiated it throughout the world.

'My policy,' Jeffrey 2 said into the battery of microphones ringing him, 'should by now be well known enough to all of you, but at least you may have a clearer picture if I elaborate it a little. As a scientist it has always been my belief that Mankind in general has misdirected his efforts. He has immense sources of power in his hands, yet invariably turns it to destructive uses. That is but one of the things which must be altered. My aim — and I freely declare it — is eventual unification of the whole world under one banner and once that is accomplished there lies ahead of us the further exploration of space, the linking up with other planets, the diversion of atomic power from potential destruction to genuine benefit — '

The roar of the crowd drowned Jeffrey 2 for a moment, then he continued again.

'It will seem to you, perhaps, that some of the methods I shall institute resemble slavery, but that, I assure you, is only because all workers must be brought under one control if we are to achieve the object ahead of us. However bitter the future years may be, however sweeping the changes, always bear in mind that it is better to slave and have progress than have freedom and yet also have to contend with possible destruction. In this day and age the menace of H-bombs and N-bombs still hangs over us. I believe that Destiny has singled me out to destroy that menace for ever.'

Jeffrey 2 said a good deal more than this, but in essence he merely repeated himself, carrying everybody along with him whilst he was on the crest of the wave. Later would come the planning and organisation, the regimentation of the country's peoples and, declared a few, the end of liberty for the individual.

Secure in his new position, the former government utterly wiped out, Jeffrey 2 thereafter set to work to arrange things exactly as he wanted them working with the added advantage of already having half a dozen men and women who were duplicates of the originals and therefore completely infallible. With utter fidelity they declared far and wide that the Leader could do no wrong, and the rank and file was compelled to agree — or suffer the consequences.

In a word, the rot had set in.

Jeffrey 2's first move was to put all the important industries of the country in the charge of his doubles, which made it look as though these beings had some say in the matter, whereas actually they were merely obeying orders they could not possibly transgress. As a result of this the country's industries were ruled by one man in the space of a month. Steel, transport, secret weapons, atomic power; all these things were his to do with as he liked.

Other countries did not like the situation at all and, as usual, immediately suspected that Dictator Dexter was planning the conquest of the world. To this his answer was that he was aiming at unification, not destruction, and that it behoved other countries to adopt a similar system to that of Britain.

Inevitably, insidiously, men and women throughout Britain found themselves conscripted for some form of labour, and not the least concession was given for domestic ties, or even for hardship caused. Jeffrey 2 was not concerned in the least how much suffering and unhappiness he caused: he was rightly determined to use men and women everywhere as workers in the first stages of his plan for eventual conquest of the entire solar system.

First he must have the whole Earth under his heel: after that the task would be easier, since it would bring to an end all 'near' opposition to his methods. So there began to appear abroad certain famous public figures who believed it would be better if every country were absorbed into Jeffrey Dexter's plan of world unification. It was, of course, absolutely incredible for die-hard government chiefs in other lands to thus declare their allegiance to a regime instituted in Britain — but there it was, and the clamour grew louder. Until finally the heads of States were compelled to go to the people and ascertain if they really desired the dissolution of their own governmental system and to come under the control of the remarkable Dexter instead.

Jeffrey 2 saw to it that the balance swung favourably in his direction and, though there were riots and small civil wars, he slowly gained his end. One after another countries came into the orbit of his very hypothetical brotherhood and unwittingly served to widen the range of his power.

In six months the world belonged to Jeffrey Dexter 2, and the only consolation in this, to Earth's teeming myriads, was that with everybody under one control war was impossible. Whether this was sufficient compensation for the burden of slavery was debatable.

The next thing, Jeffrey 2 decided, was to achieve the colonisation of Earth's neighbour worlds, and the surest way to do that was to squander Earth's resources in a mighty all-out effort. On the surface, the idea to spread throughout space was an odd one, but although without heredity, Jeffrey 2 was still at root a biological creature, and subject to the one basic biological imperative: propagation. In time the Earth would become overcrowded. Colonisation of the solar system was therefore the next logical step.

Multiplication of himself and his many doubles and dupes was the simplest thing possible — and there was no known biological limit to the number of reproductions possible.

Scientists were ordered to work out the best methods for using atomic power to drive spaceships more efficiently than existing dangerous chemical rocket methods, and astronomers and space agencies were told to supply the very latest information concerning the Moon and Mars, the first two bodies marked down by Jeffrey 2 for colonization. The facts known already were not sufficient. Every detail needed elaboration. After that, whether they liked it or not, vast numbers of men and women would be selected to form the nucleus of the colonies.

The scientists and astronomers did exactly as they were told because they were afraid to do anything else. The great mass of people throughout the world bent to their labours because they could not as yet discover any way to free themselves.

And those who had been so insistent on making Jeffrey Dexter dictator of Britain cursed the hour when the notion had occurred to them. This particular dictator was like all the rest of them — concerned only with his own advancement to the detriment of everybody else.

There were two sections of the community, in Britain at least, not affected by the titanic upheaval which had come about in the social structure, and these were those in prison and the members of the police force. Dexter had decided to ignore prisoners for one particular reason; he did not wish the release of Helen for, as a worker, she might cause a good deal of trouble, since she was a woman with a bitter grievance. It was an example of crushing the nut with a sledgehammer — leaving all prisoners as they were for the sake of one — but effective just the same. And the men of the law he did not interfere with so as to make it look to the public that he wanted justice above all. But it was in this very move that he miscalculated, for Detective-Sergeant Hanbuy was still at

Scotland Yard and he was still working with Chief-Inspector Grantham.

And by this time Hanbuy was perfectly satisfied that Grantham was not the same man as the Grantham he had known. He did everything in a curious dreamlike way; he often forgot some of the most vital points, and he openly applauded the Dexter regime whereas he had formerly been dead against any form of government which even hinted at dictatorship. Convinced of this fact, therefore, Hanbuy only needed some form of proof that he could make public, then there might arise that rebellion which was the only thing now capable of overthrowing Jeffrey 2's invincible position.

Proof? That would not be easy. Since the new regime had come there were countless exclusive agents of Jeffrey Dexter scattered about the planet, all of them alert for and ready to ruthlessly exterminate any sign of malcontents. Hanbuy knew this. He was also a trained detective and gifted with endless supplies of patience. One day, somewhere, he would find what he wanted. He did not know it but he was the only man in the world who had guessed Jeffrey Dexter's secret — and so far he was *alive*, where all the others who had known the truth had been wiped out.

Hanbuy made no sudden or precipitate moves. He continued his normal job with dour thoroughness, affecting not to notice that his superior was now completely without the touch which had made him a first-class chief-inspector. But in his spare time he endeavoured to fit pieces into the puzzle, often helped in this by pretending to be on official duty when a Dexter official questioned him as to why he was in a certain place.

It was only after nearly four months of fruitless searching for evidence of Dexter's duality that a much simpler idea came to him — so simple he wondered why he had not thought of it before. It would mean a good deal more patience and careful watching, but if it succeeded it — it *must* succeed. It was the only way to get action.

Definitely Hanbuy was a brave man, though he probably did not realise it.

Alone, he was throwing everything he knew against a non-human who had swiftly subjected the entire human race. His one hope of success, once he had the proof he needed, lay in his belief that men and women everywhere would back him up, worn out as they were by perpetual toiling to the obscure end of mastering the solar system — in which they would certainly not benefit anyway.

A year after Jeffrey 2 had come to power Detective-Sergeant Hanbuy was ready. His first move was to seek audience with Jeffrey Dexter 2 himself, and after a good deal of procrastination the interview was granted. In these days Jeffrey 2, during his 'working hours', occupied the topmost office in one of London's greatest buildings, designated now as the headquarters of world control.

Jeffrey 2 could not register surprise, otherwise it would have been evident when Hanbuy was shown into his office. The detective-sergeant's name had been forgotten long since, but not his face., Jeffrey 2 remembered it immediately.

'Take a seat, sergeant.' He motioned to

a chair. 'I seem to recall seeing you at the Yard about a year ago, during that time when my wife was in such trouble.'

'That's correct, sir.' Hanbuy seated himself, an odd little smile about his powerful mouth. 'And thank you for granting me this interview.'

'I granted it because I gather you have something of importance to relate. I would ask you to make it brief; I am extremely busy.'

'I can very soon explain, sir. In a certain place, known only to myself, there are three men. They are probably the most important men in the world.'

'How so?'

'Every one of them is *you*!'

Jeffrey 2 remained completely immobile. 'I find that very interesting. I trust also that you realise what a dangerous predicament you are in?'

'I know exactly what I am doing. Ever since you murdered Chief-Inspector Grantham — who was as dear to me as a father — I have been thinking up ways to expose you. Grantham knew your secret and so did Sir Gerald Ransome, whom you also probably murdered. I was never told by Grantham that you had a duplicate man system, nor did I ever have any proof that you might be a copy of the original Jeffrey Dexter. I have had nothing to go on except Mrs. Dexter's own passionate declarations — and I am now willing to believe that she spoke the truth. You are not Jeffrey Dexter, but some scientific freak bent on the enslavement or destruction of the human race.'

'You are too perceptive a man to remain a detective-sergeant, my friend. You must become an Assistant Commissioner.'

'Maybe I will, in a better era than this. For the moment I intend to call your bluff, Mr. Duplicate Dexter. I intend to undo everything you have done and expose you as the killer you are. In fact, I intend to put everything back on even keel, and see to it that Mrs. Dexter is handsomely compensated for the heartache and incarceration she has suffered.'

'Thank you for being so candid about your plans.' Jeffrey 2 stared frozenly. 'Apparently you have not taken into account that I have all the power in the *world*, and you have none!'

'I beg to differ, sir. I have three aces! I have three Jeffrey Dexters! It has taken me not far short of a year to locate each one of them and imprison them — somewhere that I alone know. A policeman discovers many useful hiding places, you know.'

Jeffrey 2 rose to his feet and crossed to the window. He stood gazing out of it for a moment, then spoke without turning.

'I have never insulted the intelligence of those who have guessed the truth by denying the facts, sergeant. Instead I have wiped them out — as I shall do with you. Had that fact occurred to you?'

'Naturally.'

Jeffrey 2 turned. 'You sit there and admit the possibility that I will kill you? Your courage is admirable.'

'Not at all. I happen to know that you won't kill me when you hear what I have to say. I have left at Scotland Yard a signed request that, should anything mysterious or violent happen to me at any time — at any time, notice — my comrades at the Yard are to go to this certain location where I have concealed your three doubles and are to release them — but not entirely. They will escort them to the nearest television station and transmit their images to all parts of the world. The public will be invited to ask what it intends to do with three dictators. And you know very well what will happen. The people only want some definite lead in order to spring into action. They want a springboard they can all understand — and three editions of the much hated dictator would provide it.'

'Quite ingenious,' Jeffrey 2 admitted. 'Killing you, then, or causing your disappearance, would probably lead to a good deal of trouble which I would find hard to subdue. I gather you must have an alternative suggestion?'

'Certainly I have. Relinquish control and disappear. You can at least save your life that way. Your doubles will not be seen by the public, I promise you. I'm serious about this, Dexter, dead serious.'

'So I gather — ' Jeffrey 2 returned

towards the desk and then asked a surprising question. 'Are you married, sergeant?'

'I am — with two children.'

'What a pity you did not include *them* in your touching signed request to your colleagues at Scotland Yard.'

It was whilst Hanbuy wrestled with this unexpected issue that Jeffrey 2 reached to the intercom phone and switched it on.

'Yes, sir?' It was a man's voice, very much like Jeffrey 2's own, and probably speaking on a private wire.

'Here is an order, Thirty-Six. Find the address of Detective-Sergeant Hanbuy of Scotland Yard. When you have done that you will go to that address and wipe out the woman and two children who are resident there — the wife and children of Han — '

'You dirty, monstrous butcher!' It was Hanbuy's shout of fury that cut Jeffrey 2 short, and in another second Hanbuy's powerful arm had slammed home a straight left. He was a strong man, and for once Jeffrey 2 was caught unawares. He keeled backwards, struck the armchair, then half toppled to the floor.

This was all Hanbuy needed to follow up his advantage. In one great bound he was across the office, slamming his fists into Jeffrey's face until a jab in the stomach winded him for a second. After that the positions were reversed and Jeffrey 2's giant strength came to his aid. With a series of calm, relentless blows he nearly reduced the hapless sergeant to unconsciousness and then stood looking down upon him.

'Recourse to emotional outburst apparently hasn't done you much good, sergeant,' he commented. 'Get on your feet.'

Hanbuy obeyed dizzily and then gave a sullen look. 'All right, damn you, you win! I'm not letting my wife and kids take the punishment for this plan of mine. Here — ' He threw down a rough sketch on the desk. 'That's the location where your three doubles are.'

'Thank you.' Jeffrey 2 put the sketch in his pocket after briefly studying it. 'Not that this makes any difference concerning your wife and children, Hanbuy. I gave the order and it will be carried out.'

'What! But — but I've called the whole thing off!'

'You should have considered more carefully in the first place. That you have decided to retract makes no difference to me. Once I give an order I never countermand it.'

Hanbuy was silent, breathing hard. Then, presently: 'I suppose you intend to blot me out as well?'

'Considering the way in which you have behaved you can expect little else. First, though, I mean to make sure that this sketch you have given me is correct. If it is not — Well, before you are eliminated you will be made to give the real facts.'

'That sketch is dead correct, and if you had any sense of decency you'd now withdraw the order concerning my wife and children.'

Jeffrey 2 turned to the door.

'We'll check on the sketch now. Go ahead of me and I would warn you that any false moves will have dire consequences for you.'

Hanbuy smiled bitterly. 'That I find pretty difficult to believe since you won't kill me until you have located your three doubles.'

'Dire consequences need not necessarily mean killing, sergeant. On your way!'

Hanbuy obeyed and was piloted to the elevator, thence out of the great building to an official car. He sat in complete silence as a wooden-faced chauffeur drove through the city traffic, the sketch that Jeffrey 2 had given him fixed on the dashboard in front of him. So at length they reached the designated spot and the car drew to a halt.

'This the place?' Jeffrey 2 asked curtly, and Hanbuy nodded.

'I'll have to show you. It's down the side street there.'

'All right. Go ahead of me as before.'

Hanbuy obeyed, and at a fair distance Jeffrey 2 followed him. Until Hanbuy presently reached a deserted building that had all the appearance of a one-time factory. At the side of it a flight of stone steps led to a basement door and he hurried quickly down them. Silent, three steps up, Jeffrey 2 watched narrowly as Hanbuy thrust a key in the door and turned it swiftly. Then he flung the door open and reached inside to the light switch.

'Keep going,' Jeffrey 2 ordered. 'I'll follow you in.'

Yet again Hanbuy obeyed and Jeffrey 2 cautiously finished the descent of the steps, a gun ready in his hand. He found himself gazing upon the cellar of a warehouse, the solitary electric light casting upon endless piles of rubbish and empty packing cases.

The door closed abruptly and Hanbuy stood with his back to it — but now, Jeffrey 2 noticed, he was reinforced by half a dozen other men who had evidently been concealed behind the cases nearest the door. And each one of them was armed.

Since Jeffrey 2 was not capable of revealing fear he just gazed, the sharpness of his eyes alone showing how completely he had been taken by surprise.

'Thought you had the better of the poor, ignorant sergeant, didn't you?'

Hanbuy asked grimly. 'I think I may lay claim to being a fair actor also. There are no duplicates here, nor have I ever seen any. As to my wife and children, they don't exist either: I merely double-crossed you to have an excuse to show you the sketch in the most natural manner possible. These men here belong to the Yard, or maybe you'd guessed that?'

'Very ingenious,' Jeffrey 2 commented. 'And what do you intend to do now?'

'Run you in as the greatest disturber of the peace that ever was! Maybe I'll become an Assistant Commissioner quicker than you think, Mr. Duplicate Dexter! Funny thing, one can devise all kinds of complicated methods to catch a dangerous devil like you — and fail; yet a simple ruse like this works.'

'Providing you get away with it, yes,' the multi-man assented. 'I shouldn't take too much for granted if I were you.'

Hanbuy gave a grim smile and jerked his head to the men who had sprung up around him.

'Take him out boys and follow the route I gave you. That way there won't be any disturbance.'

There was no doubt that Detective-Sergeant Hanbuy had worked everything out quite admirably, and from the look of things the ruler of the world had nose-dived straight into the trap. In less than fifteen minutes he was being escorted into Scotland Yard and there charges were preferred against him for suspected murder. Hanbuy knew he was taking a terrific gamble from the legal point of view, but having got this far he meant finishing. Accordingly the quite unmoved Jeffrey 2 was transferred to custody, there to await trial. This task accomplished, Hanbuy, after consultation with the Assistant Commissioner, wasted no time in informing the Press of what had happened.

But the news of the Leader's arrest never reached the papers. It was stopped in its tracks before it could be printed with a threat from the Leader himself that any such publication would render the paper concerned liable to instant withdrawal. Instead, an emergency radio bulletin was given by the Leader himself in which he stated quite clearly that certain enemies of the regime had invented a *coup d'etat* in the hope that it would sway a certain section of the populace against law and order.

The most astonished man in London was probably Hanbuy when this news broke. He went immediately to the cell wherein the Leader had been imprisoned and found him still there, lying on his bunk gazing unconcernedly at the ceiling. Then came an irate command from the Assistant Commissioner, and Hanbuy found himself called to explain himself.

'This morning,' the Assistant Commissioner said bitterly, 'I was inclined to think you were a man of genius, sergeant — a man destined for great things in the Metropolitan Force. I even thought of you as the liberator of a much-oppressed human race by your clever ruse in running the Leader into custody. Now we find you are completely wrong! You've bungled it somewhere, and all we have is a double!'

'But he *can't* be, sir!' Hanbuy insisted, clenching his fists. 'He was in his headquarters office when I got there, and he never moved out of it, either.'

'And what does that tell us? He knew you were coming to see him: you'd asked often enough for the interview. What was to prevent him installing a double in case you attempted something dangerous to his person?'

'Well, nothing I suppose — ' Hanbuy made the admission slowly, frowning to himself. Then a thought seemed to strike him and his eyes gleamed. 'The position is still in our favour, sir. The Leader has spoken on the radio, and a double of his — presumably — is in custody. Suppose we arrange it so that the Leader speaks on television to explain away this arrest of his and we arrange to televise his double at the same time? What will the people think about that? Don't you see that the one lever we have is to let the world at large know that the Leader is not one man alone, but several. Once we've rammed that point home everybody will know for certain that he's some kind of scientific freak and rise up against him!'

The Assistant Commissioner was a

man of experience, and certainly not one to be stampeded. After a few moments' thought he shook his head slowly.

'I feel we must find something more subtle than that, sergeant. We're dealing with dynamite now the Leader knows the lengths to which we are prepared to go — '

'Another thought occurs to me,' Hanbuy broke in, during a brief pause. 'It is possible that the man we have in custody is the Leader, whilst the one who has issued the radio bulletin is one of the duplicates.'

The A.C. gave a sigh. 'I wish I could feel as convinced as you do, sergeant, that these doubles are possible! We haven't the remotest evidence of it. It's all your hypothesis, and you could be wrong.'

'But I'm not, and I base my contention on what I have discovered concerning my superior, Chief-Inspector Grantham. He is not Grantham, sir, but a living image. I'm absolutely sure that the duplication theory is correct: I also believe that there is some way in which the Leader can control these duplicates — either of himself or anybody else — though I'm not scientist enough to be able to reason out all the details. If we accept that part of my argument it becomes obvious that the radio bulletin recently given might have been the work of a double under the mental control of the man we've arrested.'

'Possible,' the A.C. admitted. 'In fact anything's possible, but the fact remains that we are up against somebody who either is the Leader, or is under his direct orders. It's more than our lives are worth to go any further at this stage.'

Long silence — then Hanbuy gave a serious glance. 'There is one sure way, sir, of making certain of our ground. If the man we have in custody is the Leader his death may — and I think *will* — cause all those under his control to collapse, since he is probably the mental mainspring. If, on the other hand, he is only one of several duplicates, his elimination will make little difference and we'll know that the man who spoke the radio bulletin is the real Leader.'

'I admire your casualness,' the Assistant Commissioner said bluntly. 'Dammit, sergeant, we can't kill off a man just like that — just to prove a theory!'

'Not just for that reason, sir: it goes much deeper. This Leader has already tricked the populace of the Earth into believing in him, and his avowed policy is to enslave everybody to the furtherance of his own ambition. If we don't stop him now while we have the chance, we never will. We've got to take a long view of the situation.'

'Maybe — but we can't kill a man who's in custody. That's plain murder and there'd be hell to pay! No, sergeant, come back when you've thought of something else. I know the situation's serious, but I also know our limits.'

'And what about the man we have in custody? What do you propose to do? Let him go free?'

'Not yet. We may think of some way to let the public know there are two Dexters: we'll have to think about it. You also have to back up the murder charge on which you've arrested him. Seems to me the whole onus is shifted to you.'

'Yes, sir.' Hanbuy rose and thought for a moment. 'I'll think it all out, sir, and report when something occurs to me.'

6

Hanbuy plays a hand

Long before Hanbuy had any chance to act, however, the Leader himself went into action. Towards mid-afternoon of the following day the Assistant Commissioner found himself visited by two iron-jawed men with a familiar insignia on their uniforms — the symbol used by the Leader's own special police force. The Assistant Commissioner immediately scented trouble, but he did his utmost to appear cordial.

'This is an unexpected visit, gentlemen. Please be seated.'

The men remained standing; then the tallest of the two took it upon himself to explain.

'We are here under the direct orders of the Leader, Commissioner. Here is his signed authority for the immediate release of the man who was mistaken for him.'

The A.C. looked at the written authority and hesitated.

'You are warned against delay,' the big man added curtly. 'Scotland Yard has covered itself in ignominy in arresting this unfortunate citizen who happens to resemble the Leader. Even more reprehensible was the story that was almost communicated to the Press, but stopped just in time. The Leader is extremely displeased, and from what he told me I think he plans drastic action in reprisal.'

The Assistant Commissioner smiled coldly. 'For your information, my friend, I think Sergeant Hanbuy, who was responsible for the arrest, did exactly as his duty dictated. As for this 'unfortunate citizen' you speak of happening to *resemble* the Leader, I would be prepared to stake my life that he is the Leader, or an identical twin.'

'Perhaps you *have* staked your life, Commissioner: that is something which only time can prove. We have a sealed car waiting and will remove the prisoner immediately.'

'Very well.' The A.C. gave a shrug.

'Nothing I can do about that with this signed authority.'

'I am also instructed to hand you this,' the big man added, and with that he jerked his head to his companion and they both left the office.

Grim-faced, the A.C. unfolded the communication which had been given him, and the more he read the contents the more he realised their infinite finality. When the legal jargon came to be sorted out it meant only one thing — Scotland Yard as an operative police force was to be dissolved and all workers connected with it dismissed. No alternative positions were suggested, so the inference was that they would become workers like the majority of people in these days. The dissolution would be absolute, from the Assistant Commissioner of the Metropolitan Force to the lowliest newcomer to the Force. Throughout the country the police would cease to exist and be replaced by units of the Leader's own watchdogs. Which, in a word, made the dictatorship complete.

Naturally it was reprisal. The A.C. had

no doubts about this — a savage blow of dissolution for the daring effort of Hanbuy that had misfired, and there was nothing the A.C. could do but issue dismissal notices to everybody connected with the Metropolitan Force, effective as from now.

Hanbuy was not particularly surprised when his own notice reached him. Indeed, he had expected something far worse. Through roundabout routes he had already learned of the secret removal of the prisoner, and he still maintained in his own mind that it had been the Leader himself.

And now what? With the Force dissolved Hanbuy was not sure which way to turn, but he still had his teeth in things and was rigidly resolved not to let go. By evening he would be on the streets, and before long conscripted into a labour gang for general work — unless he could show very good reasons for exemption. What possible move could he make now to further his private war against the Leader?

It took him about an hour to think of a

possible line of action, an hour in which he apparently worked at his corner table in the office, dealing with a matter of importance. At the end of this time he took two sheets of paper across to Chief-Inspector Grantham 2 as he sat meditating at his desk. He had been in this silent mood ever since receiving his dismissal notice, but unlike him — or rather most unlike his original — he had not raised the slightest protest. Now he looked up as Hanbuy stood before him.

'Well, sergeant?'

'These just want your signature, sir — duplicate statement for the Errol case.'

'Errol?' Grantham looked vague. 'Oh, yes — ' He gave a brief glance over the top copy and signed it but — as Hanbuy had hoped — he gave no more than a glance at the second copy before he appended his signature.

He assumed quite naturally that it was a duplicate copy and let it go at that.

Only it was *not* a duplicate copy. It was original typing, but with the set-out of sentences very much the same as the top copy. In truth it was nothing more than a signed release for Helen Dexter. Hanbuy had once again taken one of his gambles, feeling sure that the habitually careless double of Grantham would not be too exacting — and the risk had proven justified. Smiling a little to himself Hanbuy put the signed release in his pocket and then left the office minus his coat. Since this was quite a normal thing for him to do on his peregrinations around the Yard headquarters Grantham 2 did not think anything of it. It only seemed to occur to him to make inquiry when an hour had passed and Hanbuy had not returned.

Nobody seemed to know what had become of him.

Nobody cared, for that matter, since everybody was on the move in readiness for departure. And Hanbuy himself was well satisfied, for by six o'clock that evening he and Helen Dexter were many miles away in the country and moving further away from the penitentiary with every moment.

'I can't quite understand,' Helen said as the sergeant's somewhat ancient car plugged along steadily through the early autumn evening, 'why Inspector Grantham saw fit to have me released. I was simply told he wanted me for questioning, and that was that.'

'The release was faked,' Hanbuy explained. 'I was entirely responsible for it — and got away with it. It must have been obvious to you for some time now that we're not heading into the city but away from it. Put quite bluntly we're both on the run, and I can't say at this stage where it will work out.'

Hanbuy put on the brakes and stopped the car, then he turned to look at Helen seriously. Her expression was equally serious. Around them was the comparative quiet of the countryside, free, for the time being anyway, of the everlasting eyes and ears of the innumerable agents of the Leader.

'Whilst you have been imprisoned, Mrs. Dexter, the whole social life of the country — even of the world — has turned inside out,' Hanbuy said after a moment. 'Yon probably know that?'

'I've heard plenty of rumours.'

'They were quite true. But I've also learned many things — and in particular I want you to know that I now sincerely believe the story you once told Inspector Grantham and myself about your husband having been murdered and replaced by a duplicate man.'

Helen smiled faintly. 'Better late than never, sergeant, but the damage is done now. This unicell creature posing as my husband is in a position of absolute power.'

'Nobody is ever that, Mrs. Dexter. There is always somebody just a little cleverer, and I'm trying to be that person. I nearly had the Leader where I wanted him, but he eluded me.' And he proceeded to a frank explanation of what had happened.

'And he'll beat you every time,' Helen said soberly, 'because all the force is on his side. The next thing he'll probably do is seek you out and kill you.'

'I rather doubt that. Not that he *wouldn't*, but I imagine he will think I can do no more harm.'

'Well, *can* you?'

'That depends on you, Mrs. Dexter. I engineered your release from prison because you're the only person who can perhaps help me in my one-man campaign.'

'I'm only too willing if it's possible. I've a big debt against the Leader for the murder of my husband — to say nothing of Hal Walsh — but I certainly don't see where I can be useful.'

'Well, we'll come to that later. For the moment our task is to find somewhere where we can hide out in reasonable safety — granting that is that you're prepared to throw in your lot with me?'

'With the world in its present state I'll take any risk. And besides, anything is better than being in prison.'

Hanbuy nodded, switched on the ignition once more and then resumed driving. Helen remained at his side her brows knitted as she strove to think of something whereby she might be able to help the reckless but determined sergeant.

It was inevitable, of course, that her 'stage managed' release from the penitentiary where she had been incarcerated as a 'mental case', must be finally discovered. The moment it was the matter was referred back to Chief-Inspector Grantham 2, who denied all knowledge of the business, and from him the affair was referred to the Leader himself. Absorbed as he was in matters concerned with the production of a mighty fleet of spaceships he would not even have condescended to consider the problem — but the name of Helen Dexter, linked vaguely with that of Sergeant Hanbuy, who had also vanished, arrested his attention.

Immediately he ordered a country-wide search to be made for the missing pair, and his agents in foreign countries were also notified to be on the alert — but week succeeded week and no clue as to the missing pair's whereabouts presented itself.

Actually, Hanbuy and Helen were not very far away — no further indeed than the wooded countryside that lay some twenty miles outside the perimeter of London itself. Nor were they alone. Hanbuy had acted on the perfectly logical assumption that there must be hundreds of men and women who had escaped the labour conscription and were just as anxious as he and Helen were to be rid of the Leader. Accordingly, a band numbering perhaps two hundred were living the lives of nomads, possessed of modern weapons which had been taken by stealth from the city — or from some unwary guard who had paid with his life for investigating too closely. Here lay the nucleus of a revolutionary army, the inevitable outcome of a regime that was daily becoming more tyrannical.

Hanbuy was the accepted leader since it had been he who had gathered together these fellow wanderers. The virtue lay in the fact that they were all of the same mind: the Leader must be obliterated, and afterwards all those who swore allegiance to him. If this were not done the total enslavement of all the human race for an unguessable time was mercilessly possible.

'But for us just to sit around here day by day, running to our underground shelters when a guard or bad weather threatens, isn't going to get us anywhere!'

Hanbuy declared one morning. 'We have got to have some kind of concerted action — and for that we don't want just a few hundreds, but thousands, and those thousands armed to the teeth! We have managed to circumvent all efforts to locate us, and we'll continue doing so, but we have got to carry this war into the enemy camp. According to the latest radio news the Leader now has the workers of every country engaged on the exclusive construction of space machines. He has also stated that in a few weeks the advance vessels will leave simultaneously for the Moon and Mars to study at first hand the conditions on those bodies. It doesn't require much imagination to guess what that may mean. The colonization of the Moon and Mars will divert vital resources from the peoples of Earth. All because of the inhuman ambitions of this creature who is not a man at all, but a travesty!'

'I always have the feeling,' Helen said quietly, sitting in the undergrowth at Hanbuy's side, 'that it is *I* who should make the major move. For one thing I have the most reason because the Leader has the physical vestment of my husband; and for another I could probably have stopped this ghastly cell experiment from even commencing had I been firmer in the first instance. I just didn't realise what was afoot.'

'I am afraid we are all sadder and wiser now,' Hanbuy commented gravely. 'However, you alone cannot do anything, Helen, nor would any of us men here even think of it. But this I *do* ask: can you not remember some of the things your husband used to tell you concerning this experiment? Never mind how irrelevant it may seem. If there is the least thing you can recall let us know of it.'

'Matter of fact I *have* made one or two notes,' Helen said, getting to her feet. 'Just a moment whilst I get them.'

She hurried away to the underground dugout that was her own particular abode, presently returning with a roughly-clipped sheaf of papers. The men and women lounging and listening in the undergrowth, all of them in clothes that were dirty and becoming sadly worn, waited with interest for what she would have to say.

'I'm afraid there's nothing very definite,' she apologised after a moment or two. 'Just odd bits which I picked up from my husband after he no longer kept it a secret that he was making a unicellular man. Here's one: 'The unicellular man is unique in that he comprises in one unit all the attributes and deficiencies normally embodied in tens of thousands of such cells — ' Then there's — '

'Just a moment,' Hanbuy interrupted, and turned his attention to the listeners. 'I've never inquired of any of you what your former occupation was. Is there anybody here who was a biologist before joining this little band?'

'I'm not a biologist by profession,' one middle-aged man volunteered, 'but I studied it a lot as a hobby. Would that help?'

'Considerably, perhaps. Where Mrs. Dexter refers to something that is essentially biological, would you mind making a note of it? I'm only trained as a police officer, and science is outside my field. But I do feel that somewhere here we may hit on something that will enable us to act decisively. Sorry, Helen, please go on.'

Helen nodded and continued: '"The actual life span of a unicell man cannot be predicted with certainty, but it is possible that he might exist throughout the span allotted to normal humans . . . The unicell man has the advantage over us because he is free of the problems of heredity . . . It is surprising to think that the unicell man, with all these advantages, is also surprisingly vulnerable. Where a normal human being suffers injury through the destruction of a group of cells constituting the thousands which make up his body, the unicell man is complete in one piece, and whatever fractures any part of that cell — which is his body — must of necessity destroy *all* of him".'

Helen glanced up. 'That last one wasn't from memory: it was one of Jeff's own notes on the subject. I've several of them here which I took from the house when I was arrested.'

Hanbuy nodded slowly, distance in his eyes. Then after a moment's thought, he said: 'Would you mind repeating that last statement again?'

Helen complied, and the man whose hobby was biology also wrote down the words in shorthand. The absent-minded look remained on Hanbuy's square face.

'It's the statement that the unicell man is vulnerable that keeps getting me,' he explained. 'I can see the point, too. If you assume that a human being resembles thousands of blown-up balloons all tied together it's easy to see that if one or more is destroyed through injury or violence, the others remain and the body, to a certain extent, can go on functioning. But if there is only one balloon, gigantic so as to measure as much as all the smaller balloons put together, then the destruction of that one would bring annihilation. A definitely crude analogy but probably most of you see what I mean?'

'You have it exactly,' the biologist said, 'and your analogy isn't so crude as you imagine, Hanbuy. To liken cell clusters to bunches of balloons is surprisingly accurate.'

'Good!' Hanbuy looked gravely pleased.

'Any more from me?' Helen questioned.

'Not for the moment, Helen. I want to sort this one out if I can. I feel it's got something. Let's see now: what is there that can destroy an entire giant cell?'

The biology hobbyist got to his feet and came across. 'Matter of act, Hanbuy, it isn't a case of that. You're just making things difficult for yourself. The vital point is: what is there destroys a *cell*? The size has nothing to do with it. What will destroy a small cell will destroy a giant one.'

'Bullets? Knives? Electricity?' Helen suggested hopefully.

The biology man nodded slowly. 'Yes, I suppose all of those things would bring instant death by shattering the entire hypertrophied cell instead of just a part of it, as in a normal human being. Only I don't see how any of us could get close enough to the Leader to use any of those methods.'

'And the Leader isn't the only unicell man or woman,' Hanbuy pointed out. 'There must be hundreds of them scattered about the world by now, and as long as they remain — even if the Leader should die — they form a deadly menace. They can reproduce so rapidly and so easily that the human race could be crowded off the Earth in a very short time. We have to think of something which will effectually destroy the lot of them, and at one fell swoop if we can manage it.'

Silence, except for the cool autumnal wind rustling the dry leaves overhead — then one of the women who had been lounging lazily in the undergrowth and looked quite incapable of prolonged concentration, made a casual suggestion.

'Atomic power. Everything seems to hinge on that these days.'

The biology hobbyist gave a start and looked sharply towards her. Hanbuy looked too, but not because anything brilliant had occurred to him.

'That's it!' the hobbyist exclaimed, momentarily astonished. 'Why the devil didn't we think of it before? May I ask what gave you the idea, madam?'

'Heaven knows.' The fat woman shrugged briefly. 'It just happened to occur to me that everything these days is discussed in terms of atomic power. I don't even know what that is so I can't claim to have said anything wonderful.'

'But you have — believe me!' The hobbyist turned back to Hanbuy as he stood trying to look knowledgeable. 'Look, Hanbuy, it's as simple as this: Atomic power necessarily includes the emanation of dangerous radiations — alpha, beta, gamma. The basis of thermonuclear fission. Correct?'

'Correct.'

'Right then. Gamma rays are used medically now and again these days to destroy rampant cells in the case of disease. And the gamma rays are so deadly they wipe out cells instantly, corrode and burn them into nothing. Gamma-ray surgery is one of the biggest advancements of the day. You're still with me?'

'Still with you. So?'

'Well, there it is. Produce gamma rays in sufficient quantity and wherever there's a unicell man or woman within range that monster cell — or man — will cease to exist. It will shrivel and die.'

'And human beings who happen to be near?'

'We cannot discriminate,' the hobbyist said quietly. 'Humans involved in gamma rays will suffer severe burns, certain cellular destruction, even blindness and insanity, but they will not be *totally* destroyed like the unicell creatures. Somebody's *bound* to suffer. The thing is to work the idea out.'

'From what basis?' Helen questioned dubiously. 'To talk of releasing gamma rays in sufficient quantity is about as possible as walking to the Moon and back. It just can't be done.'

'It has *got* to be done — somehow,' Hanbuy said. 'It's the answer we've been looking for and it's up to us to make it work. Gamma rays — gamma rays. Let's see now — '

'We don't need to concentrate on gamma rays exclusively,' the hobbyist said. 'If we can only release sufficient atomic power we'll get those anyway — along with alpha, beta, X-rays, and all the rest of them. The problem is where to find enough atomic force. It exists in two places — controlled in the world's power stations and uncontrolled as A, H and N bombs. And we haven't the remotest chance of getting at any of those sources.'

'At the moment it looks that way,' Hanbuy admitted, sighing, 'but I shall continue to think about the problem just the same. Somehow a way's got to be found.'

It was only after several days, however — days mostly spent in hiding from the emissaries of the Leader as they investigated these remote parts outside the city area — that a solution presented itself to Hanbuy, and it was such a surprising one that even he held back at first from mentioning it. Then, finding no other alternative, he gathered the members of the 'outlaws' together m the wooded clearing and explained.

'I see nothing else for it, my friends, but to make the Leader start a war!'

There was an astonished silence for a moment or two, then Helen looked at Hanbuy sharply.

'But surely that's the very thing we don't want? Even world slavery is better than war. At least everybody stands a *chance* of overthrowing the Leader as long as they remain alive. Once war starts it will finish everything.'

'Besides,' one of the men remarked, 'there couldn't be less justification for war than there is now. The Leader has unified all nations under one control: the only war there could be would be occasioned by the revolution of the masses, and there isn't the faintest possibility of that.'

'Rumours of it would be sufficient to accomplish two things,' Hanbuy continued. 'It would force the Leader to launch an attack in order — so he believed — to get his body blow in first and crush impending attack; and it would also bring an interruption in his nearly completed plan to send spaceships to the Moon and Mars and waste natural resources. The only way to start war is for me to go into the lion's den and name a series of danger spots which the Leader should attack.'

'But, for heaven's sake, what *good* will it do?' Helen demanded, horrified. 'You'll inevitably lose your life; you'll start a war — and civilisation will probably finish. What kind of plan do you call that?'

'I call it the *only* plan, Helen. In launching war the Leader will throw into it everything he's got — every type of atomic bomb that exists. We know the effective radii of such bombs, so all that I need to do is name supposed secret hide-outs corresponding to the radii of the bombs' effectiveness and the entire Earth will be involved in their deadly radiations! Tens of thousands of innocent human beings will die, certainly, because we have no means of warning them — but it is also certain that probably every uni-man and woman on the face of this planet will be instantly destroyed. The few that escape can be dealt with afterwards. Drastic ills need drastic remedies. The sacrifice of the innocents to destroy the unicellular creatures is our last chance of ever regaining freedom.'

'Damned if you're not right,' the

hobbyist muttered after some thought. 'The only thing I jib at is the annihilation of the innocents, but that can't be avoided. I can foresee one grim possibility, though: that the Leader may be aware what atomic radiation will do to him and his kind and therefore fail to drop into the trap. There is also the almost certain possibility that he'll surround himself with radiation-proof walls. Then where are we?'

'As long as I can stay alive I shall use every trick I can think of to stop him saving himself,' Hanbuy said. 'Naturally there are snags to every plan, but this one is the only one we can put into operation.'

'And for you it means certain death,' Helen said. 'We can't let you do that! There must be another way — '

'There isn't. I've thought the problem out from every angle. Nor am I inclined to regard my death as such a certainty, either. The Leader will not be rid of me until he thinks he knows every hideout. In any event I intend to take the risk. The best thing the rest of you can do is get as far underground as you can and steal as much lead as possible with which to line your retreats. The fireworks are going to be pretty violent when they do start.'

With that Hanbuy turned away, his mind made up. A few calls of good luck and God speed followed him, then as he reached the edge of the clearing Helen caught up with him. She took hold of his arm earnestly.

'A moment, Hanny.' Her eyes searched his square face intently. 'You seem to have forgotten something. I'm in on this as much as you are.'

'That's plain silly, Helen. No need for both of us to take the chance of losing our lives.'

'As far as I am concerned I'm not bothered. There's nothing much to live for in a world like this — and with Jeff dead too. Even if most of us survive after the war that is coming, I'm not too keen to take part in the rebuilding. Life died for me on the night Jeff was murdered.'

'The fact remains,' Hanbuy replied slowly, 'that I refuse to take the responsibility for leading you into a death trap. And, speaking selfishly, I prefer to work unhampered. You'll find there is a lot to live for later on.'

'But, Hanny — '

'No, Helen.' He clapped her affectionately on the shoulder. 'Be a good girl and leave it at that, eh?'

With that he went on his way across the meadow that skirted the wood. Helen watched him go, but she made no attempt to follow him. He had said he preferred to work unhampered. She watched him until he was out of sight, then slowly and reluctantly she turned back to join the others. But in her heart of hearts she still wanted to help. It was not that she had any love for Hanbuy — that was enshrined in the memory of her husband — but she was convinced that she ought to take some part in bringing about the downfall of the man who was her husband's double. The odd thing was that it never dawned upon her that she had already done all that was necessary by quoting a vital sentence from Jeffrey's notes.

And Hanbuy, for his part, did not waver for a moment in his intentions. He kept on going towards the metropolis, and long before he reached there he found himself overtaken by guards, questioned, and thereafter escorted. Not that this mattered since it was exactly what he had expected. Also, as he had expected, the Leader had given orders that he was not to be dealt with by ordinary methods, but must be brought before the Leader himself.

So, in less than an hour after leaving his colleagues, Hanbuy found himself in the Leader's office atop the executive building.

'It has taken quite a time to locate you, sergeant,' the Leader commented as completely without emotion as ever.

'I wasn't located. I came deliberately — and to refer to me as 'sergeant' with the police force dissolved is rather pointless, isn't it?'

The Leader shrugged. 'As you wish. So you came deliberately? From that I can only assume that you wish to commit suicide.'

'Anything but it. The truth of the matter is I found that living like an outlaw amongst a mob of disorganised and utterly useless citizens was too much for me. I'm a man of action, as you know already.'

'Oh yes, I'm quite aware of that. Nobody but a man of action and extreme audacity would have imprisoned the Leader as you did, or have engineered the release of Mrs. Dexter so neatly. You have certain qualities that I find quite admirable. The pity is that they arc directed on the wrong side.'

'It would be more correct,' Hanbuy said quietly, 'to say that they *were*. The fact that I have returned to the city, to virtual capture, surely is sufficient indication of a change of heart?'

'Perhaps. Knowing your ingenuity I would prefer something more concrete. You don't expect me to believe that you just came back to offer your services, do you? You must have more behind it than that.'

'I have, yes,' Hanbuy assented, seating himself without being asked. 'I've travelled around a good deal since I made myself scarce and I also came into contact with many 'cells' of unrest. From unrest there has come organised force, and out of that will come revolution.'

'And you are a spokesman for the revolutionists, no doubt armed with the necessary audacity to think you can make terms with me?'

'I make no terms, and I am not one of the revolutionists. I know they cannot win against you, and I prefer to be on the winning side. As a guarantee of good faith I will show you exactly where the various headquarters of these revolutionaries are. Knowing that there is nothing to prevent you obliterating them — '

The Leader reflected, which made things decidedly difficult for Hanbuy. He was quite unable to tell from the Leader's expression what he was thinking. The inscrutability was absolute.

'I admit that, for once, I am puzzled,' the Leader confessed, getting lo his feet and musing. 'On the face of it your proposition sounds like a complete *volte face*, a complete reversal of allegiance. I cannot help but try and delve for something deeper, the reason why you have made such an extraordinary proposition.'

'I have no ulterior motive,' Hanbuy lied, shrugging.

'You realise that, if I so decide, I shall blast these various revolutionary headquarters out of existence?'

'Certainly I realise it. You will make total war on the revolutionaries before they can make war on you. That suits me perfectly since I've no wish to be with them. Now I have had time to think I've come to the conclusion that your way of running things is far and away better than anything a normal human being could do.'

The Leader gazed. Perhaps he was puzzled, perhaps suspicious; it was impossible for Hanbuy to tell. But now he had launched the business he kept on going.

'I have a proviso to make regarding my revealing the whereabouts of these various headquarters.'

'Ah! Now we come to it! Well?'

'I want all my past misdeeds wiped off the account. Let me start fair and square on your side — and in an official position. You have very few normal humans who work willingly with you, I imagine — so one like myself who really wants to can be invaluable. I know so much about the people.'

Silence. The Leader was still obviously trying to reconcile matters to himself.

7

Atomic vengeance

'Very well,' the Leader said abruptly, 'I'll take a chance on your proposition, Hanbuy — not so much because I trust your change of heart, but because of the possibility that you may be right in what you say about revolutionary activities. I cannot afford to ignore danger to my authority. I assume these various headquarters you mention are scattered in various parts of the world?'

Hanbuy nodded, then getting to his feet he went across to the huge map of the world on the opposite wall and singled out various points. The fact that each one was separated by roughly two hundred miles — the effective area of the latest thermonuclear bombs — did not seem to occur to the Leader.

'But there are hundreds of them!' he exclaimed. 'You don't expect me to believe that you have contacted each one of those in the past few weeks, do you?'

'I have only contacted a few of them, from which I learned of the others.'

'I see. Very well, our best move is to take a fast jet plane and study each of these areas at close quarters.'

'And be shot down?' Hanbuy shook his head. 'I wouldn't advise that.'

'You mean these revolutionaries have the necessary weapons?'

'They have — in almost every instance. Your only hope is to use remote-controlled planes and have them drop everything they have got on each one of the headquarters simultaneously. I know that will involve a good deal of organisation and pinpointing of targets, but it's the only answer. Sudden and total annihilation is the only sure action.'

The Leader spent a few moments studying the various potential targets. Then: 'Simultaneous attack as suggested will involve the entire land surface of the planet. That will inevitably mean the destruction of all cities either from direct hit or else blast. It's a high price to pay. I have everything perfectly organised and smashing it all down is not an agreeable prospect.'

'Wrecked cities can soon be rebuilt,' Hanbuy said; and with a flash of inspiration added: 'Regimes cannot. Better to be sure you've destroyed all possible chance of revolution and use the survivors to build up a better-organised civilisation. As it stands, cities and towns are cramped and old-fashioned anyway. A world clearance is long overdue.'

The Leader returned to the desk and sat down. 'For a normal human being possessed of emotions you certainly take a ruthless viewpoint, Hanbuy, don't you? You've counted the cost in losses? Tens of thousands of useful workers will perish. Tens of thousands more will be rendered maimed and useless.'

'I am aware of it,' Hanbuy said, his square face solidly resolute. 'I can only urge that you do not delay.'

'I shall move as I deem fit, Hanbuy — and *when* I deem fit. I cannot do anything until I have made the necessary provisions to protect myself and those most valuable to me. The storm of radiation which will be released from so many thermonuclear explosions simultaneously will be stupendous.'

Hanbuy did not say anything. He was busy cursing himself for an idiot for ever having thought that the Leader would overlook the necessity of protection.

'And,' the Leader finished, with an ominous stare, 'there is also the matter of yourself. You made the proviso that I should forget everything you have done. I did not say that I accepted that proviso — nor do I. You have shown me where these vital places are, therefore I have no further use for you. You would be better out of the way, Hanbuy, for I cannot rid myself of the conviction that you have some deep motive for wishing to stay at my side. I am unable to find what it is, so I will adopt the safer course of wiping you out.'

Hanbuy felt his pulses race. It also meant that his gamble for his life had failed. He had played all his cards in the hope, even in the belief, that the Leader would grant his one request — but he had underestimated the complete lack of conscience the unicell man possessed. All right, so now he was fighting for his life.

'You have no guarantee,' he said, forcing himself to sound calm, 'that the headquarters I have indicated are the right ones. I would be a fool to give you all the answers right away, would I not?'

'Even if you are wrong by hundreds of miles, bombs of high calibre in the areas indicated will take care of the situation. I believe you *did* give the right headquarters and trusted to luck that I would comply with your proposition.'

Hanbuy shrugged. 'Very well. Against you I am powerless, but there are many things you'll regret if you kill me off. I haven't told you everything by any means. Destroying the various headquarters would not necessarily mean the absolute end of all revolutionary possibilities.'

'No? What else could there be?'

Hanbuy took a shot in the dark. 'You have been building hundreds of space machines for the intended colonisation of Mars and the Moon. Do you believe for one moment that every worker is so browbeaten and controlled that he hasn't the initiative to put together the plans of the space machines' design? Search through your records of workers throughout the world engaged on spaceships and you will find probably a hundred missing. By various secret means they have eluded guards and surveillance and escaped into the void with half a dozen spaceships.'

'Absurd!' the Leader snapped. 'The guards would have immediately reported such a happening to me.'

'And perhaps incur the death penalty for negligence? Hardly!'

The Leader demurred. Hanbuy took a deep breath. For the moment his handout of falsehoods had kept his life intact.

'Assuming you are right,' the Leader said presently, 'I do not see it signifies. The loss of half a dozen spaceships amongst thousands doesn't mean a thing!'

'Not even when those ships are equipped with the very latest long-range missiles? Those men who have ventured out into space can easily target their missiles towards Earth — and they will at a given time unless stopped by a secret radio call sign.'

'They can be sought out and destroyed!'

'You think so? They can see the moment ships leave Earth to look for them, but those who leave Earth cannot see them against the black of space. No investigators will ever find them.' Hanbuy hunched forward. 'I know where they are, Leader, and it is my signal which will prevent them hurtling destruction down upon Earth. They do not know I have changed sides and come over to you. If I die that signal will never be given, and what your bombs on headquarters miss, the missiles will complete.'

'You can be made to reveal the nature of that signal, Hanbuy. I have effective means of persuasion.'

'And have somebody else give the signal? It must be in my own voice or it will not be heeded.'

'Under persuasion, Hanbuy, your voice could be recorded!'

'I know, but it is part of the signal that the position of certain stars must be mentioned at the same time. That would not be possible unless I spoke at the psychological moment.'

The Leader relaxed. Hanbuy's face was so wet it looked as if he had raised it from a bowl of water and forgotten to dry it.

'Very well, you win,' the Leader said abruptly. 'How much of what you have told me is true I don't know, but I am in the position that I dare not take chances. I shall, however, take the precaution of putting you under protective arrest until I am ready to go into action. As I said, every precaution must first be made to safeguard ourselves — especially those who are of a like physique to myself.'

Which could only mean, Hanbuy realised, that the Leader was wide awake to his vulnerability as a single cell.

'I will see to it that you are given a room and every courtesy, until such time as I decide what must be done with you.'

The Leader pressed a button on his desk and presently a guard appeared. For Hanbuy it was the end of the interview and of the hardest fight he had ever put up to stave off certain death. The guard was given brief instructions, and before long Hanbuy found himself in one of the most comfortable suites in the executive building. Here at least he would have a chance to think further in case another battle of wits became necessary to save himself from death.

Meanwhile the Leader went into action. He issued orders to the countless underground and surface workshops constructing spaceships, suspending all work thereon and instead diverting the labour forces to the top-speed construction of underground atomic shelters. In many cases the workshops themselves were converted for this purpose. Nor was this all the Leader did. From the astronomers he demanded to know if there was any sign of half a dozen space machines somewhere between Earth and Mars, or Earth and the Moon. To which the astronomers politely but coldly rejoined that the most powerful telescopes on Earth could not pick up six space machines even if they were there.

The Leader was not satisfied with this. In fact he was not satisfied that Hanbuy had told the truth in the first place — so he gave immediate orders for a space machine to be launched into the void, its navigators to discover, if possible, the location of the supposed six space machines.

Since the crewmen were slave human workers, thrown into this hazardous undertaking without so much as a 'by-your-leave', they never came back. Days passed into weeks, during which time the shelters were rapidly brought to completion, but no word came out of the void, nor did the machine return. To the Leader it meant only one of two things — either the investigators had been overwhelmed, as Hanbuy had predicted they would be, or else they had flown straight across space to either Mars or the Moon in preference to returning to Earth and slavery. Either way the Leader was no nearer, and most certainly he did not dare to get rid of Hanbuy — not yet.

Altogether it took several months to provide the required shelters, and all of these were to be used by the unicell men and women and one or two human beings who, like Hanbuy, were of extraordinary usefulness. The remainder did not matter. The Leader knew full well that the problem of workers and population simply did not exist when multiplication by fission was so easy.

Another week passed whilst worldwide arrangements were made in secret for the exodus below, and if the workers wondered what all the preparation was about they were not given the slightest clue. That they did not start to revolt was something that surprised the Leader: he had expected it long before this. Since it did not come he went ahead with the next stage of planning — the deployment of the various air forces who would simultaneously drop their loads of thermonuclear explosives on the positions indicated by Hanbuy on the world map.

It was only after the organisation of the air forces was completed that trouble arose. Pilots, checking with each other, very soon discovered that they would all be dropping their loads at approximately the same time. What chance, then, had they of escaping afterwards? The bombs would all be exploding as they tried to make their getaway. Whichever way they turned they would fly into radioactive clouds and probably certain death. So the Leader found himself with a deputation of grim-faced pilots to deal with.

'We can put the case quite simply, sir,' the spokesman said. 'Every one of us refuses to accept the assignment. It's nothing better than suicide!'

'If you don't do it you'll be overwhelmed by the biggest revolution ever known on this planet,' the Leader stated. 'Which way do you prefer to die — by the myriads who oppose my regime or by the radio-activity involved in their destruction?'

'Guided atomic missiles would do just as well,' another of the pilots put in.

'I do not agree. That allows a margin for error, and in a case like this there must be no error. Nothing but an overwhelming blow at every fester spot simultaneously.'

The spokesman, a human being, knitted his brows. 'Do I understand you to mean, sir, that we are striking these blows at the heart of a revolutionary movement?'

'That is correct. Whether you agree with

the revolutionary movement is beside the point. You are part of my air force and have your orders. If you refuse to obey them you know the penalty. There are other pilots who can take your places.'

'Not a case of that sir,' the spokesman said. 'I'm just wondering where these revolutionary spots are supposed to be. Surely not the places we've been ordered to bomb?'

'Certainly!'

'Then it doesn't make sense, sir. I know three of the spots referred to in this country because I did my training there up to a few weeks ago. There certainly wasn't a sign of revolutionary movement then. Either above or below the ground. Part of our training was underground for practice in atomic defence.'

The Leader hesitated, thinking. Then: 'You are sure of this?'

'Perfectly sure, sir. It is not my place to inquire where your information concerning revolution came from, but if the other supposed 'fester spots' are as harmless as those in this country I fancy no revolution is possible.'

The spokesman pilot did not add 'unfortunately', though it was pretty clear from his expression that he thought it.

'You can go,' the Leader said abruptly. 'I shall withhold my orders for the moment. Return to your bases until you hear from me.'

The pilots went on their way without further words, and the Leader turned to the intercom on his desk. As the result of what happened in the few hours which followed Hanbuy found himself summoned to the Leader's office — and the expression on the multi-man's face was sufficient to warn him that something had gone desperately wrong somewhere.

'You have been playing a most extraordinary game, Hanbuy, haven't you?' the Leader asked deliberately.

'Game? I don't play games, Leader. The world's in too grim a mess for that.'

'I'll put it another way. You invented hundreds of mythical danger spots which were all going to attack in unison unless I destroyed them.'

Hanbuy was silent, wondering what was coming next. He knew soon enough.

'I accepted everything you said at its face value because I felt sure you meant it. Now I know you were lying! No danger spots exist. I have had investigation made of all the points you mentioned, and there is absolutely nothing to be found — nor any trace of there having been revolutionary headquarters at an earlier date. You relied on the fact that I would not make such an investigation — that I would attack from the air with overwhelming force, using up valuable stocks from the atomic pile to no purpose. I can only think that the reason for your wild plan was to halt the progress on space machines.'

'At least,' Hanbuy said quietly, knowing the battle was lost, 'it was worth a try.'

'I have also had space investigated in an endeavour to discover the six space machines you mentioned. The attempt led to nothing because the investigators never returned — so whether you were lying in that instance as in the other I have no idea. I can well believe that you were. You know what this means, Hanbuy, don't you?'

'Yes, I know, but killing me won't avail

you anything. You'll wish you hadn't.'

'I am prepared to risk that,' the Leader retorted, and with that he turned to the buttons on his desk. After a moment an armed guard entered and the Leader glanced towards him.

'Take this man away and transfer him to the lethal chamber. Inform me when sentence has been carried out.'

Hanbuy went — without a word, the helpless victim of a gamble that had not come off. That same day, towards the close of the bleak autumn afternoon, the radio bulletins callously announced that former Detective-Sergeant Hanbuy of Scotland Yard had been 'liquidated' for treasonable offences. To the majority who heard the news it meant nothing; but to Helen Dexter it meant a great deal. She, along with the rest of the roving band who were by now in a deep underground shelter lined with lead — in accordance with the instructions Hanbuy had given them before his departure — looked fiercely around her on the troubled faces as the news bulletin ended.

'Well, what are we going to do?' she

demanded. 'Sit here and take it? Sergeant Hanbuy had the courage to try and defeat the Leader — twice in fact — and now he's paid the ultimate penalty. It's time for the rest of us to show our loyalty to the cause he instituted.'

'Doing what?' asked the biology hobbyist, switching off the portable radio. 'Hanbuy was a clever man, as well as a brave man, and I'm sure any technique we could evolve for hoodwinking the Leader just wouldn't work.'

Helen moved restlessly back and forth in front of the very inadequate oil stove.

'The trouble is that we don't know how far things have gone,' she muttered. 'We know from the radio that spaceship building was stopped in order to provide shelters — but that's all we *do* know. Is the Leader going to do the bombing which Hanbuy outlined to us, or not?'

'I'd say not,' one of the men remarked. 'Hanbuy must have slipped up somewhere, so it's more or less certain the Leader found out he was putting forward a phony scheme. I'm reasonably convinced that the bombing onslaught won't come off.'

'Which will mean, perhaps, that the protective shelters may be pulled down again.' Helen pondered for a moment. 'Can we by any chance make use of that fact? Can we turn this setback into a resounding victory?'

'I'm afraid nothing short of a miracle will accomplish that,' the hobbyist commented dubiously. 'In fact, Helen, I just don't grasp what you mean.'

'I mean that it wasn't to our advantage to have the Leader and the rest of his minions inside shelters when the bombs went off! That would have defeated our intentions anyway, because they would all have escaped the radiations. If only we can engineer a sense of false security; let them pull their shelters down, and then strike! That is what Hanbuy would have wanted us to do.'

Grim silence. None were as relentlessly determined as Helen to destroy the Leader and all he stood for. But then they had not lost so much at his hands.

'I'm not stopping here, inactive, waiting for something to happen to give us a chance,' Helen declared finally.

'I'm going to do as Hanbuy did — even as I should have done at first. I'm going to the city to find out all I can, to try and finish the scheme that Hanbuy started. He must have made some headway, and I mean to find out how much.'

'Which means you'll walk right to your death as he did,' one of the women pointed out. 'That's plain crazy, Helen.'

'Crazy it may be, but I'm going to do it. It doesn't matter to me whether I die or not — So here I go.'

Nor did Helen waste a moment longer. She hurried to the door of the hideout, slipped on the stolen overcoat that she had made her own property, and within minutes she was outside in the cold, drizzling dark of the autumn night. Far away in the distance the lights of the city were shifting and winking through the rainy blur. Helen gave a little shiver and then started moving, squelching through the thick mud of the clearing that had replaced the undergrowth of the warmer days.

Before long she was on the windswept meadow bordering the wood, bending her head against the rain. As she tramped onwards she tried to devise in her mind some kind of plan that would give her convincing reasons for returning to the city. Not knowing what kind of story Hanbuy had told she was considerably at a loss to know how to —

Abruptly she realised that there was a different sound around her. It was no longer the soft whistling of the wind and the faint hiss of the increasing downpour in the mud. It was a whirring, rushing note, like a plane descending rapidly with its engine cut off. Perhaps it was a plane?

She stopped and looked about, but beheld no sign of aircraft lights. And the sound grew louder — and louder yet — so much so that she instinctively crouched in the expectancy of something suddenly descending upon her. No such thing actually happened, but she was able to briefly glimpse a darkly gleaming shape sweeping down some hundreds of feet above her, its wet metal sides reflecting the lights from the city. Then with a distant concussion that made the ground tremble briefly the object landed.

Helen straightened and stared in amazement through the murk. It seemed impossible, but the thing had looked exactly like a spaceship. Definitely it had not been an airplane. She began running even as she asked herself these questions, and in less than five minutes had come upon the great metal vessel deeply embedded in the mud. Its portholes were lighted, a fact that Helen had not noticed earlier in the mist of rain.

Cautiously she moved again until at last she had manoeuvred into a position where she could see through the lowest-placed porthole. She fully expected to behold fantastic other-world creatures beyond, but instead there were four men, grim-faced, absolutely Earthly, having about them the resolute toughness of travellers to alien lands.

For Helen the mystery was complete, but certainly her curiosity was much greater than her fear. Raising her hand she hammered forcibly on the densely thick glass, but even so it was quite a while before one of the men noticed her. Immediately he said something to his colleagues, and one of them nodded towards the airlock.

Wondering, but not particularly afraid since she was amongst men of her own world, Helen stepped through the aperture as the airlock was opened, and then gazed in fascinated interest around the control room.

'You — you speak English?' she ventured at last.

'We should,' one of them replied dryly. 'The lot of us were born in London.'

'But — What are you doing in *this* thing? Where have you come from?'

'Space. Or, to be more specific, Mars. We couldn't resist it.'

'Then this is a private ship of your own?'

One of the men, square shouldered and hard eyed, shook his head.

'This is one of scores madam. The Leader sent us into space to look for a group of space machines that he thought were threatening Earth. We couldn't find 'em. We found space so intriguing we decided to go further — hence we went to Mars and had a brief look round. Then back we came to report. And from the look of things we landed pretty close to London. Difficult to see the way on a night like this. None of which explains what you're doing here.'

Helen did not answer the question. 'You mean the Leader literally forced you to go into space?'

'That's it. We got the idea we might stop on Mars and never come back here — but the idea didn't work out. Mars is dry as dust with a devilishly thin and poisonous atmosphere. Earth, Leader or no Leader, is a better spot.'

'And have you radioed the Leader's forces to tell him you were returning?'

'No — because we're in something of a dilemma. Having disobeyed his orders in diverting to Mars, we're worried about reprisals. We landed here to try and work out our next move — '

'It goes without saying, I suppose,' Helen asked slowly, 'that none of you are loyal to the Leader?'

Three of the men grinned sourly. The fourth was more elaborate: he spat on the metal floor.

'Give us one chance,' one of them muttered, 'and we'd cut the heart out of the dirty swine! But that's hoping for too much: he's got everybody under his thumb and things look likely to staying that way. Unless there's been some alteration whilst we've been away?'

'There nearly was,' Helen said, sitting on the nearest screwed-down chair. 'I may as well tell you all about it since you're obviously on my side. I'm an outlaw, one of a band of men and women who are dedicated to the overthrow of the Leader. One of our number nearly did it.'

'He must have been a genius,' growled the man who had spat. 'Tell us about it.'

Helen did so, in detail, and the men listened in complete attention. They were thoughtful for a while after she had finished.

'That man Hanbuy had a good idea,' one of them said. 'In fact, a damned good idea. And it's the first time we knew that the Leader and a lot of his cohorts are not normal human beings. No doubt of the fact that the atomic radiation plot would have finished the lot of them at one blow had it come off.'

'But not with them in protective shelters,' Helen insisted. 'For that reason it's perhaps just as well the plot failed. I am clinging to the hope that there may still be a way to produce the atomic blast without these creatures being able to protect themselves.'

'And you hoped to accomplish that by yourself?' one of the men asked in wonder. 'One woman against the Leader and all he stands for?'

Helen smiled faintly. 'A mouse can stop a powerhouse if it happens to short-circuit it. Just the same, I'm glad to have fallen in with you men. Perhaps you'll have better ideas on the subject?'

'Yes,' one of them muttered. 'Forget the whole thing. We can't win against a creature who's just a travesty of a human being.'

'Don't be too sure,' snapped the one who had spat and who apparently was the self-appointed commander of the group. 'This man Hanbuy started something which mischance prevented him finishing. As Mrs. Dexter here says, there might still be a way. The answer to the problem is obviously atomic force, and Hanbuy worked out a way to make the radiations worldwide. With that scheme scotched what else have we?'

Apparently nothing, but the other men did not say so. They looked thoughtful instead, and Helen waited too, anxiously, her eyes on the big man who was the commander. Then abruptly a thought seemed to strike him.

'There are five of us here, and if we can't get an idea between us it's a pity. It also occurs to me that as yet the Leader probably doesn't know we've returned to Earth. The moment he does know he'll be nailing us down as before. If we hop hack into space before we're spotted it'll give us time to decide what we're going to do.'

Decision, as far as the commander was concerned, meant instant action. The airlock was closed and Helen looked about her in some trepidation, by no means sure what kind of an experience the take-off would be.

'Use half power,' the commander ordered as his colleagues moved to the various controls. 'For one thing it'll make things easier for Mrs. Dexter, and for another we won't betray ourselves by too much exhaust.' He turned and looked at Helen. 'I'd advise you to lie on that wall bunk over there, madam. You'll find easy to use straps. Take the strain off your heart.'

Helen promptly obeyed, and for the next few minutes, as the power plant whined, she wondered if the end of the world had come. The breathtaking speed and sense of downwardly bearing pressures as the vessel leapt through the storm clouds and into the clear void beyond was something she never wanted repeated.

Then, gradually, she sat up, aware of the amazing lightness of her body. The view outside the porthole compensated her for the rigors she had undergone — only there was not time for her to dwell at leisure on the wonders of outer space. For the next hour she followed the directions of the Commander in orientating herself — as best she could — to the weightless conditions of freefall, as the vessel fell into an orbit around the Earth. Eventually she managed to 'sit' a few inches above her bunk, holding on to one of the many grips scattered throughout the vessel.

'I suppose,' the commander said, looking across at Helen, 'you don't happen to know if Hanbuy ever got far enough to detail the air force to bomb the chain-explosion points he had in mind?'

'No idea at all. That was one of the things I was going to try and find out.'

'Somehow we must find out,' the commander decided. 'The air force as a whole is as much against the Leader as everybody else. If we could let them know privately the reason for the intended bombing assault I think they'd carry it out. If by some chance they were detailed to such a task — and then had it cancelled when the Leader presumably found out about Hanbuy's double-crossing, all the better.'

'Walt Sherstone is the nominal head of the air force,' one of the other men remarked. 'Or at least he was when we left Earth. One of the Leader's big-shots is the official Air Marshal, but Sherstone is the one with the men behind him, and in charge of actual operations in the field.'

'And Sherstone knows me well,' the commander mused. 'We even trained together at one point in our careers. Now if I could only contact Sherstone I'd get to know a good deal as to how the land lies.'

'One way of doing it,' said the man beside the switchboard, 'is send a message in ordinary air-training code. If the Leader picks it up, which isn't very likely, he'll probably not understand it. Certainly he won't be expecting anything suspicious because as far as he knows we haven't returned from outer space.'

'Yes, it's worth chancing,' the commander admitted, and wasted no more time. Punting himself to the radio equipment he switched it on and began issuing the call sign used the world over by the air-training squadrons. Whether it was still used now the Leader had taken over the air force was something the commander had to risk — and the risk came off, for presently an answer came through the speaker, crystal clear even though the spaceship was some hundreds of miles from Earth's surface.

'A.T. answering. State your communication, please. Over.'

'Urgent message for Captain Sherstone. Over.'

'May be delay finding Captain Sherstone. Stand by — '

Those within the space machine waited expectantly, exchanging anxious glances and wondering if the Leader would once again discover that a move was being made against him. Then suddenly a sharp, matter-of-fact voice came through.

'Captain Sherstone speaking. What is your communication?'

'Walt,' the commander said calmly, 'this is 'Shirty' Morgan. Remember me?'

'Hell, of course I do! Why this means of renewing an old association?'

'It's the only means, that's why — and it's a gamble too, in case the Leader hears.'

There was a sound rather like a dry chuckle. 'That isn't very likely, Shirty. The air-training radio bands are on a special frequency and only air-training receivers can pick them up. The Leader ordered the air-training wavebands to be done away with long ago. We obeyed — but created a different frequency. It's our one means of contact with each other in different parts of the world. If the Leader ever finds out it's the finish, but so far he hasn't.'

'Couldn't be better!' the commander exclaimed with a quick glance at the delighted faces around him. 'Now fix yourself for a surprise: I'm speaking from outer space, several hundreds of miles from Earth. I have with me three colleagues from the workers' section and one lady — Helen Dexter.'

'Space? Helen Dexter? You don't mean the wife of the Leader?'

'That's a long story — and here it is.' The commander telescoped the details as much as possible and then came round to the real reason for his communication.

'I can definitely confirm,' Sherstone replied at length, 'the Leader *did* detail the air force to release thermonuclear explosives on a number of selected targets, but the pilots discovered that if all their bombs went off at once they'd be committing suicide. They wouldn't be able to get clear of radioactive clouds and dust quickly enough to escape death. They told the Leader they refused to commit suicide — and for some reason he never pressed the matter. Maybe he found out afterwards that the targets were just duds.'

'More than likely — but the point is, Walt, how far was this simultaneous bombing programme advanced? Had a plan of action been worked out? And the atomic bombs assembled?'

'Of course — to the last detail and bomb. It was then that the pilots discovered it was a suicide job.'

The commander was grimly silent for a moment, then: 'How many of them would still be prepared to take on this suicide job if they knew it would mean the end of the Leader and the rest of his blasted unicell cohorts?'

'Not very many, I'm afraid. These air force boys are not cowards, Shirty — but they're not fanatics either. They haven't suffered as much at the hands of the Leader as the workers have, so they've less reason to desire violent retaliation. I very much doubt if more than half a dozen would agree to still carry out the bombing plan.'

'This is damnable!' the commander snapped. 'An entire plan has been worked out and that man Hanbuy died so it could be worked out. Dammit, don't they realise what this swine of a Leader will do if he keeps on having his own way?'

'I don't think they even think about it, Shirty. I for one can't blame 'em if they don't want to kill themselves just yet.'

The commander sighed. 'Well, that kills everything. Nothing more we can do, so — '

'No, no, wait a minute!' Helen exclaimed, her eyes bright. 'Don't switch off yet; I've got an idea.'

'Yes?' The commander looked at her without much confidence.

'Can this spaceship travel at speed in atmosphere without burning up? I don't know much about science, but I do know atmosphere causes a lot of retardation to speed, and tremendous friction.'

'Those *were* serious problems for the early spaceships,' the commander conceded. 'But all of the latest modern craft have a revolutionary protective coating that negates friction. We can't do much about retardation, but even so we could fly through atmosphere at many thousands of miles an hour — ' he broke off, puzzled. 'But why on earth should we *want* to? The whole idea of a spaceship is to get out of the atmosphere and into space as quickly as possible!'

'But what if you need to circumnavigate the world?' Helen persisted.

'We simply go into space and fall into an orbit, like we're doing now.'

'But you *could* go lower, and fly like an aircraft?' Helen's eyes narrowed in thought.

'We could,' the commander acknowledged. 'But why should we want to, anyway?'

'Don't you *see*?' Helen insisted. 'These air force men don't want to do the job, but *we* could! Our surprise attack and the speed at which we'd move would stop anything catching up with us — unless another spaceship were suddenly launched after us, but by then we'd have done the damage — '

'You mean,' the commander interrupted, 'that we drop the bombs on the targets in a non-stop run round the world?'

'Yes!' Helen's eyes were bright. 'Captain Sherstone can probably discover what the targets were — '

'The targets don't matter,' the commander interrupted, catching something of Helen's enthusiasm. 'Just as long as we drop bombs at intervals so as to make their radii of effectiveness overlap, the thing's done. A chain of them round the Earth — like sowing peas. You've got it, Mrs. Dexter! It's the idea of the century.'

'Can't we just drop the bombs from orbit?' one of the crewmen asked. 'That way we'd circumnavigate the Earth a hell of a lot quicker.'

'No, that's out of the question. Dropped from orbit, the bombs would be travelling at tremendous speed when they hit the atmosphere. They would burn up with friction long before they reached the surface — and being atomic, they wouldn't explode, either.'

'There's still the matter of getting the bombs,' Helen said, hesitating. 'And also the apparatus, or whatever it is, for dropping them.'

'Say, Shirty, I'm still here!' came the voice of Captain Sherstone through the loudspeaker. 'And from what I've been overhearing it sounds as though outer space has sharpened your wits up a good deal. As for the bombs and releasing them, to the best of my knowledge they're still in air force care, in storage. And I should be able to contact some of the scientists and technicians who were going to travel with the air crews to prime and release the bombs before the scheme was aborted — '

'Then you think the scheme's good?' the commander asked quickly.

'Definitely! And moving at a speed faster than any conventional aircraft, you'll be clear of all blasts before they can affect you.'

'They can't affect us in any case,' the

commander answered. 'This spaceship, like the rest of them, is insulated against all radiations. It has to be in order to fly in the void where radiations abound.'

'Good enough! And we'll do our part down here as near as we can. I'll get all the reliable men I can and if there is any sign of the Leader trying to stop your whirlwind onslaught we'll intercept the interceptors if at all possible.'

'And the bombs and their operators?' the commander asked. 'We have to rely on you for those.'

'I'll see we get them somehow. Here's what you do. At midnight tomorrow night you'll see a signal light to the north of the main out-London training grounds. Descend there and collect: we'll see everything's ready.'

'Done!' the commander exclaimed.

'And one other thing. Be more sensible, don't you think, to let the Leader dismantle every shelter and subside into false security before you start the atomic blitz? That will also give us time to warn as many innocents as possible to save themselves.'

'Yes, that makes sense,' the commander agreed. 'Providing those who are warned don't give the game away and ruin everything.'

'I'll use my discretion, Shirty; you can be sure of that.'

'Right! Midnight tomorrow. Meanwhile we remain here in orbit and bite our nails with impatience.'

* * *

Helen in the hours which followed, could find no possible flaw in the plan of which she had thought, and she was more than gratified that her own unexpected ingenuity had at last allowed her to think of something which would catch the ruthless twin of her husband on the hop. In fact, for the first time since the ghastly night when she had realised she was alone with Jeffrey's duplicate, she felt reasonably content. A master plan had been devised; she was amongst men who treated her with the respect her sex deserved; and down below on Earth a resolute air force captain was doing everything he could to make the plan foolproof.

So the hours passed, the space machine orbiting just beyond Earth's telescopic range. Helen even found time to absorb the wonders of the void. Then at last the commander set the machine on the move again, sweeping down from the everlasting blaze of the sun towards the Earth, then heading in the direction of the night side until at length the sun was lost to view and the vessel plunged lower and lower into the murk of the winter night.

Finding the signal light — visually and by radio means — was only a matter of normal aircraft navigation, and finally the commander brought the vessel down silently out of the cloudy sky and made a perfect landing no more than a quarter of a mile from where the signalling apparatus was in action. This done, it was only a matter of moments before the airlock was opened — and the first person to come through it was the rotund, uniformed figure of Captain Sherstone himself. Once the preliminaries of introduction were over he turned quickly to the commander.

'Everything's fixed,' he said briefly. 'I've got the men ready to load up your hold with all the bombs necessary to blanket the world, and the scientists to prime them.'

'And have you managed to warn those who don't need to be involved?' Helen asked quickly.

'I've started the ball rolling, Mrs. Dexter, but it will be a week or two before the warning has spread to its safe limits.'

'A week or two? But we can't wait that long!'

'I think we can,' the commander said with a grim smile. 'With every day that passes the Leader is moving more and more protection from himself and his minions and thinking less and less of possible attack. The best thing, Walt, will be for you to radio us when you think the time is ripe for attack.'

'I'll do that,' Sherstone promised. 'Now I must be going and see how those lads of mine are faring with the bombs. Best of luck, all of you. If ever there was a single overwhelming blow for freedom, this is going to be it.'

With that he went on his way, and for the next hour, whilst members of the air-training forces kept on the watch for possible interruption, the deadly cargo was loaded into the spaceship's hold, supervised by Captain Sherstone and scientists and technicians who would be going on the flight.

And finally it was completed. Again came the good wishes and the handshakes and the return into the void, accomplished on half power as before, both for the sake of saving Helen too much distress and to disguise the tell-tale rocket exhaust. So into outer space, that endless vacuum where the machinations of thinking beings and their lust for power seemed so utterly trivial and pointless.

The vigil had begun, and the one link with Earth was the radio. From the news bulletins it seemed clear enough that the Leader and his many minions had not the least idea of the plot against them. There appeared to be no change in policy. The shelters were still being torn down, many of them being converted into the giant spaceship workshops which they had originally been. Work on spaceships was to be resumed immediately, and hours were to be lengthened to catch up on lost time. This was a bad move on the Leader's part, for it made those who wavered in the hint and whisper campaign being directed against him suddenly decide to throw in their resources to oppose him. Everywhere the word was being spread amongst the oppressed: they could have freedom if they would but follow directions.

The directions came primarily, of course, from Captain Sherstone, and as he had expected none of the workers betrayed whatever information was given them: they hated the Leader too much to step out of line for a single moment. It was not therefore difficult to gradually herd the more important of the workers — skilled craftsmen who would he needed in the rebuilding of civilisation — to regions which were lead-proofed and deep underground, provided with all the necessities to withstand a long siege. Of these moves the Leader knew nothing. He was too busy working out plans for the colonization of the Solar System; and in any case there was no normal human being loyal enough to him to give a hint of what was really happening.

Then at long last, just when those aboard the spaceship had begun to feel that they could wait no longer, Captain Sherstone gave the go-ahead order. He made it brief since he too had a good deal to control down on Earth, and he also had himself to protect from the rain of destruction to come.

'Right,' the commander said, his face grim. 'This is it! We all know what we're going to do, and if we make it it's the finish of the Leader and the entire unicelled mob that supports him. Jim — that ejector mechanism okay?'

'Entirely.' Jim prepared to move into the corridor. 'I've tested it so often to make sure I could operate it with my eyes shut.'

'Maybe — but don't. Keep the bombs concentrated on land areas. No point in wasting them in the ocean. Harry, you've computed the course we're taking?'

'Check! Everything worked out.'

'Bob, you're all set to watch for possible attack?'

'All set, chief.'

'And the bombs are all primed to detonate on impact?'

'They are,' the head scientist assented. 'And the sooner we've got rid of them the better I'll like it.'

'Very well, then.' The commander took a deep breath and settled himself at the control board. 'Here we go, and our prayer is that Providence will see us through to the end of the journey.'

'We'll come through,' Helen said quietly, settling in her bunk. 'What we are doing is absolutely vital to the liberty of the individual.'

The vessel was brought out of orbit, and its speed decreased as it fell through the atmosphere. The eternal external silence was rent by the mounting scream of riven air as the machine flashed lower and lower. Its exterior glowed fiery red, but inside the insulated hull the temperature remained unchanged. Nevertheless those inside began to sweat with the sheer tension of the situation.

The vessel turned and began to sweep downward in a mounting power dive, straight towards the mighty globe of Earth spread below.

With everything perfectly rehearsed, the commander straightened out the vessel at exactly the right moment now flying parallel with the Earths' surface at a height of two miles. Since it was a clear, cloudless morning there was no doubt that the vessel had been observed. Possibly even now the astounded Leader was being informed that the travellers who had gone into space had at last returned.

Then the first bomb went down. Its frightful power released itself when the space machine, flashing onwards at thousands of miles an hour was already parting with its second bomb. Light beyond imagination blazed evanescently from the explosions, and behind them came the smashing, disintegrative walls of deadly radiations and supercharged gases. The third bomb went down, and from then on it was a repeated dropping of the terrifying cargo in a straight line across the world.

Not once did the vessel falter in its steady velocity; not once did Jim miscalculate in the dropping of the bombs. This was ruthless, absolute destruction, and not until every bomb had been dropped was the commander prepared to call a halt.

What sort of ghastly confusion was reigning on the world below Helen could only guess at. The spaceship was always well ahead of the explosion preceding. But eventually, at the end of some two and half hours, they dropped the last bomb and came within sight of the inconceivable havoc that the first bomb had produced. Huge areas were in flames: there was a stupendous crater where the bomb had dropped, and the highest point of the atmosphere was charged with radioactive dust and discharge.

And this was an envelope that was spreading everywhere, masking the battered, tumbling world beneath. The commander did not even stay to look, but headed out into space again — and there remained as, day by day, Earth remained clouded over, the hell below completely masked.

Then at the end of a week a message came through. It was from Captain Sherstone.

'Okay — come home! We've a safe shelter at north point ground. You *did it*! There isn't a unicellular being alive *anywhere*!'

THE END

Books by John Russell Fearn in the Linford Mystery Library:

THE TATTOO MURDERS
VISION SINISTER
THE SILVERED CAGE
WITHIN THAT ROOM!
REFLECTED GLORY
THE CRIMSON RAMBLER
SHATTERING GLASS
THE MAN WHO WAS NOT
ROBBERY WITHOUT VIOLENCE
DEADLINE
ACCOUNT SETTLED
STRANGER IN OUR MIDST
WHAT HAPPENED TO HAMMOND?
THE GLOWING MAN
FRAMED IN GUILT
FLASHPOINT
THE MASTER MUST DIE
DEATH IN SILHOUETTE
THE LONELY ASTRONOMER
THY ARM ALONE
MAN IN DUPLICATE
THE RATTENBURY MYSTERY
CLIMATE INCORPORATED

THE FIVE MATCHBOXES
EXCEPT FOR ONE THING
BLACK MARIA, M.A.
ONE STEP TOO FAR
THE THIRTY-FIRST OF JUNE
THE FROZEN LIMIT
ONE REMAINED SEATED
THE MURDERED SCHOOLGIRL
SECRET OF THE RING
OTHER EYES WATCHING
I SPY . . .
FOOL'S PARADISE
DON'T TOUCH ME
THE FOURTH DOOR
THE SPIKED BOY
THE SLITHERERS
MAN OF TWO WORLDS
THE ATLANTIC TUNNEL
THE EMPTY COFFINS
LIQUID DEATH
PATTERN OF MURDER
NEBULA
THE LIE DESTROYER
PRISONER OF TIME
MIRACLE MAN

Other titles in the
Linford Mystery Library:

F.B.I. SPECIAL AGENT

Gordon Landsborough

Cheyenne Charlie, Native American law student turned G-Man, is one of the Bureau's top agents. The New York office sends for him to investigate a sinister criminal gang called the Blond Boys. Their getaway cars somehow disappear in well-lit streets; they jam police radios; and now they've begun to add brutal murder to their daring robberies. Cheyenne follows a tangled trail that leads him to a desperate fight to the death in the beautiful scenery of the Catskill Mountains . . .

DR MORELLE MEETS MURDER

Ernest Dudley

Here is another collection of the strange adventures of Doctor Morelle. The sardonic detective's cases include: an hotelier killed with a brass candle-stick; a Baroness poisoned with cyanide; a diamond robbery, and the shooting of zoologist Professor Raymond. The doctor, in his inimitable cerebral style, also investigates: a fake suicide; the stabbing of the wealthy Mr Franklyn; the ex-prisoner accused of murder, and the strangled film star. All whilst aided — or handicapped — by his gentle, timorous assistant, Miss Frayle.